A CHILLING VISION . . .

A sound interrupted Johnny's thoughts—a clashing, banging noise. Johnny peered around through the gathering darkness, and then he saw it: The door on the empty cabin had come open, and it was hitting against the cabin's metal wall as the ship rolled, making a nerve-racking noise. Quickly he padded across the deck and grabbed the steel door handle. He was about to slam the door shut when he peered into the lighted cabin.

There was somebody . . . no, rather, it seemed to be some*thing* . . . sitting in one of the seats. It looked like a scarecrow. Its back was to Johnny, so he couldn't tell if it had a face, but it was wearing an odd sort of carroty red wig, and it was dressed in some sort of white coarse shirt. Johnny was puzzled. Why on earth would anyone bring a scarecrow onto a ferryboat? And just then, while he stood there wondering, the ship rolled gently, and the scarecrow lurched to one side. Johnny looked down, and he saw the scarecrow's foot sticking out into the aisle.

It was a skeleton foot. A cluster of white bones.

THE SPELL OF THE SORCERER'S SKULL

THE SPELL
OF THE
SORCERER'S SKULL

JOHN BELLAIRS

Frontispiece
by Edward Gorey

A BANTAM SKYLARK BOOK®
NEW YORK · TORONTO · LONDON · SYDNEY · AUCKLAND

RL 6, 008–012

THE SPELL OF THE SORCERER'S SKULL

*A Bantam Book / published by arrangement with
Dial Books for Young Readers*

PRINTING HISTORY

*Dial Books edition published November 1984
Bantam Skylark edition / November 1985
9 printings through October 1988*

*Skylark Books is a registered trademark of Bantam Books,
a division of Bantam Doubleday Dell Publishing Group, Inc.
Registered in U.S. Patent and Trademark Offices and elsewhere.*

ISBN 0-553-15726-4

Published simultaneously in the United States and Canada

---

*Bantam Books are published by Bantam Books, a division of Bantam Doubleday
Dell Publishing Group, Inc. Its trademark, consisting of the words "Bantam
Books" and the portrayal of a rooster, is Registered in U.S. Patent and
Trademark Office and in other countries. Marca Registrada. Bantam Books,
666 Fifth Avenue, New York, New York 10103.*

PRINTED IN THE UNITED STATES OF AMERICA

CW   18   17   16   15   14   13

The Spell of
the Sorcerer's Skull

CHAPTER ONE

"Phooey! Phooey on winter and snowy white snow and jingle bells and walking in winter wonderlands! Bah! We should never have come up here in the first place!"

It was a cold February night in the year 1952, and snow swirled around the picturesque white houses and the sprawling old Fitzwilliam Inn in the beautiful little New Hampshire town of Fitzwilliam. It whitened roofs and the grass of the town common, an oblong park that the town was built around, and fell on the heads and shoulders of two people who were trudging slowly around the common. One of these was a short, red-faced elderly man, Professor Roderick Childermass. He had a strawberry nose and wildly sprouting muttonchop whiskers, and he was wearing a battered, shapeless fedora and a threadbare and dirty tweed overcoat. His hands were jammed into the pockets of the coat, and as he stomped along, he kept making bad-tempered comments. Walking next to him was a pale, bespectacled boy named Johnny Dixon in a red stocking cap and a blue parka and galoshes. Johnny was shy and nervous-acting. He kept looking anxiously at the professor, and every now and then he would open his mouth to say something. Suddenly he would change his mind and stay silent.

"Winter paradise indeed!" snorted the professor, glancing fiercely this way and that. "I'd like to give a piece of my mind to the boneheads who settled up in this godforsaken wilderness! *And* to the cheapo types who run the state and don't provide enough money to clear the roads or sand them in the wintertime!"

"Please, professor!" Johnny said in a mild, placating voice. "Don't be angry, please, don't! Everything'll be all right! It really will, you'll see! We've got a room at the inn for tonight, and they're towing your car right now. It's not so bad, really it isn't! And I'm having a good time. The town is wonderful, and I like the inn a lot, and I like going places with you. So don't worry—it'll be all right!"

The professor stopped scowling. He turned and smiled kindly at Johnny, and then he reached out and patted him on the shoulder. "Well, as long as you're not *too* disappointed," he said. "I'm sorry I lost my temper, but I get wrathful every time I think of that slippery road, and us skidding and sliding into that ditch! I wanted to show you New Hampshire in the wintertime, and it really is quite beautiful in the snow. We were having a good time, and then that dratted accident had to happen!" The professor paused. He turned and looked across at the large shadowy inn on the far side of the common. Its windows glowed yellow, and smoke curled from the tall chimneys. All around the common, houses were filled with lamplight. Candles winked in the darkness here and there. Snow swirled everywhere, and was piling up on gateposts and ledges and roofs. It was a lovely, dreamy Christmas-card scene.

"Ah, well," said the professor. "I suppose things *could* be worse!" A gust of wind hit him, and he shivered. "Brrh! But it is getting *cold* out here! How about it? Shall we head back to the inn and have a nice hot drink by the fire before we turn in? I think a hot toddy or a brandy or two would improve my disposition immensely."

Johnny agreed, and they started back. As they drew near to the inn, they heard the grinding sound of an engine, and, turning to their left, they saw a tow truck crawling up out of the dark hollow behind the inn. Hanging from the tow chain was the professor's maroon Pontiac. Its right headlight had been gouged out, and the right front fender was a shapeless mass of dented, squashed metal. The two travelers watched solemnly as the tow truck rolled past. Again Johnny shot a glance at the professor, and he was relieved to see that the old man was taking things calmly.

Johnny liked the professor a lot. He had met the professor a little over a year ago, right after he came to live with his grandparents in the city of Duston Heights, Massachusetts. At the time he had been scared and lonely: his mother had died recently, and his dad had gone off to fly a jet in the Korean War. Later his dad had been discharged from the Air Force, but he had re-enlisted because the Air Force had needed his special skills as a pilot. The professor had befriended Johnny, and his friendship had been like a wonderful gift: he played chess with Johnny, taught him to bake cakes, and went places with him. He argued with him about war and politics, and really listened when Johnny tried to give his opinion about something. For a shy kid who was used to being ignored by grown-ups, this was really something incredible. Johnny was proud to be the professor's friend, and he was willing to forgive him when—every now and then—the professor lost his famous temper.

A little later the two of them were relaxing in one of the parlors on the first floor of the old inn. It was a cozy room, with its cushiony armchairs and sofas, frilly-shaded floor lamps, and faded, tattered red Oriental rug. A fire was roaring in the fireplace, and its light flickered over old dusky paintings and a gilded banjo clock with a brass eagle on top. The professor was sitting in a saggy armchair by the fire with his shoes off and his feet propped up on a low footstool. In his hand was a glass of brandy, and he was smoking one of his black-and-gold Balkan Sobranie cigarettes. His eyes were half-closed, and the look on his face said that he was at peace with the world. Johnny was standing over by a low bookcase in a corner leafing through some of the books. He was trying to find one that would be fun to read in bed.

The professor sipped his brandy and smiled blissfully. "Aaah!" he said. "Sitting around and doing nothing is one of the great underrated pleasures of life! Tomorrow I know that I will have to do something about that wretched car, but right now I wouldn't move a muscle to save it if it was about to fall off a—"

"Hi there!" said a friendly, rumbly voice by the door. "Can I come in and join you guys?"

The professor and Johnny turned and looked. It was the owner of the inn—a man about sixty years old, with grizzled gray hair and a leathery, seamed face. He wore a plaid shirt and a saggy, unbuttoned woolen sweater, old stained work pants, and battered hiking boots. He was smoking a pipe and leaning against the doorpost with his arms folded across his chest, looking very relaxed and at home.

"Of course, of course. Please come in!" said the professor, motioning with his hand. "There's an extra chair here, right by the fire, and it *is* your inn, after all! Have you met my young friend, John Dixon? He's my partner on this ill-fated northern expedition."

Mr. Spofford walked across the room and shook Johnny's hand warmly. Then he went to the armchair that stood near the professor's and sank into it. He leaned back and stared at the fire, puffing his pipe for a minute or two. He looked tired, and was obviously glad to have a chance just to sit and catch his breath for a bit.

After a few more minutes of silent meditation, Mr. Spofford turned and smiled at the professor. "They get your car outa that ditch okay, did they?"

The professor nodded glumly. "Yes, they did. I'm going over to whosis' garage tomorrow morning to see if it will be possible to drive the filthy heap of rust back home. But for now, I'm just glad to be here, safe and sound."

"Glad to have ya, glad to have ya," said Mr. Spofford pleasantly. He leaned back and blew a stream of smoke at the mantelpiece. "I see by the way you signed the guest book that you're a professor, Mr. . . . Mr. . . ." He paused and grinned apologetically at the professor. "I'm sorry. I hate to admit it, but I couldn't read your handwritin'. Mine's nothin' t'brag about, but yours is worse. Is it Chilmark or Chillingsworth or what?"

The professor glared at Mr. Spofford. His handwriting was awful, and he knew it, but he hated to have people comment on it. "It is Childermass," he said stiffly. "Roderick Childermass, Ph.D."

Mr. Spofford looked shocked. His hand flew to his mouth, and there was an uncomfortable silence in the room. Johnny was bewildered. He glanced from one man to the other. What on earth had happened?

The professor set his brandy glass down on a table by the armchair. He stubbed out his cigarette in an ashtray and folded his hands in his lap. "My dear sir," he began, coldly, "there are a few traitors and renegades in our family history, but on the whole, Childermass is an ancient and honorable name. There was a Childermass at the battle of Agincourt, and another with the barons who forced King John to sign the Magna Carta. So may I ask why my name has given you such a turn?"

Mr. Spofford gave the professor an embarrassed sidelong glance. "Oh, it ain't nothin' against . . . against you personally. Or . . . or your family name. It's only jist that, well, we got this clock here that we show to visitors sometimes, an' it's s'posed to be haunted, an' . . . well, it's called the Childermass clock."

Now it was the professor's turn to be astounded. His mouth dropped open, and he looked positively aghast. "Good Lord!" he said, in a slow, awestruck voice. "So *that's* what became of it!"

At the word *haunted* Johnny's eyes lit up. He had been listening to this conversation with growing interest, and now he was totally fascinated. "Hey!" he exclaimed. "Is it really haunted? And . . . and can we see it? I'd really like to . . ." His voice trailed off. Embarrassment overcame him, and he wondered if maybe he had said something he shouldn't have.

The innkeeper glanced quickly at Johnny, and then he turned back to the professor. "Do . . . do you *know* about this darned thing? I mean, why it was made and what it's for, an' . . . an' everything?"

The professor sighed. He picked up his brandy glass,

swirled the liquid inside, and took a sip. "Alas, yes," he said gloomily. "I know far too much about that clock. And I wouldn't be a bit surprised to hear that it was haunted. Not one bit. So it's here! Good gravy! It was stolen when the old Childermass place—our family home, up in Vermont—got broken into about ten years ago." The professor paused and smiled wryly at Mr. Spofford. "I assume," he went on, "that you wouldn't have told me about the clock if you had been the thief yourself. So would you mind telling me how in blazes it wound up here, at this place?"

Mr. Spofford shrugged. "No. I wouldn't mind tellin' you. It's a weird story, though: y'see, it got left on the front porch here, one night durin' a snowstorm. Next mornin' my wife stuck her head out the front door, an' there 'twas, with a piece o' burlap sackin' pulled over the top of it. No note with it, er nothin'." Mr. Spofford paused and stared at the fire. "Somebody musta wanted t'get rid of it," he added in an odd tone of voice.

There was a brief silence. Johnny could hear the banjo clock ticking and the fire crackling. Suddenly Mr. Spofford leaped to his feet.

"*Well!*" he said a bit too loudly. "Would you two like t'see the darned thing? How about it?"

Johnny said yes, he'd love to see the clock, and the professor agreed. They followed the innkeeper out of the parlor and around a couple of corners, and then down a wide hall that ran from the front to the back of the old building. On their left rose the staircase that led to the second floor. On their right were closed doors. Mr. Spofford opened a door at the far end of the hall, and he flipped a light switch. Johnny and the professor found themselves in a small disorderly room full of broken or unused pieces of furniture. There were cane-bottomed chairs with the seats smashed out, and end tables with broken legs. Against one wall was a stout workbench with a vise clamped to one end, and next to it was a dusty library table. On the table stood the clock.

It was quite large for a shelf clock: two feet wide and about four feet high. The case was made of dark, close-grained wood that shone with varnish. The upper half of the clock was a lot like the shelf and mantel clocks that were made by the Willard Brothers of Massachusetts back in the early 1800s. There was a churchy pointed "roof" on top, and it was flanked by two carved wooden spires. The face of the clock was made of white painted metal with black numerals, and the hands were of curly, fancy cast bronze. Painted neatly on the face were the words *M. Childermass fecit* and the date 1889. In the bottom part of a clock of this sort, you usually saw a pendulum behind a square glass door. But in this case, what you saw was a dollhouse room. It was made to look like the parlor of a well-to-do Victorian house of the 1870s or '80s. Everything was done very carefully in miniature: when Johnny squatted down and peered into the shadow-box room, he saw a red Turkish carpet on the floor and an oval antique table with a green plush cover. On the table were an oil lamp, a pair of glasses, and a Bible.

Next to the table was an old-fashioned easy chair, upholstered in black leather. On the left was a fireplace, with candlesticks and a mantel clock, and against the rear wall was a sideboard with two tiny wine decanters on it. Above the decanters hung an oil painting in a gilt frame. A fussy, curly backed, red velvet sofa stood against the right-hand wall, and near it a door stood ajar, showing a cloak and a top hat hanging on pegs in the hallway. The wall to the left of the fireplace had a built-in bookcase, and before it stood a doll that was made to look like an old man. It had a silky gray beard, a black suit, and a black string tie. The doll appeared to be studying the bookcase, and its hand was stretched out in the act of taking a book from a shelf.

Johnny and the professor squatted down, with their heads close together. They peered into the room, taking in all the odd, intricate details.

"Over there—look at that!" said the professor, pointing a long, tobacco-stained forefinger. "Those things on the shelves on the left side of the fireplace. Aren't they marvelous?"

Johnny looked at the row of built-in shelves. Instead of books, these shelves held objects: teeny baskets of fruit, a set of scales, a wine bottle, and a skull.

"That skull has always kind of fascinated me," said

the professor, reaching farther into the room. "It was brought back from California by my granduncle, and I suppose that it is ivory, or maybe it's bone. At any rate, it's a very curious little doojigger, and cleverly made, but I cannot for the life of me figure out why my father decided to put it into this room. After all, the room is supposed to be an exact replica of the study of our old family home up in Vermont, but there was never any— ah!"

With a sudden indrawn hiss, the professor jerked his hand back. The tip of his finger had accidentally touched the miniature skull.

Johnny was alarmed. "What is it? What's wrong?"

The professor examined his fingertip curiously. "Hmm . . . Well, there's nothing wrong, actually. I just got the oddest sensation from touching that skull. But I suppose it's all my imagination—there seems to be no harm done."

"Cut yourself, did you?" asked Mr. Spofford, stepping forward.

"No, no—nothing of the sort!" said the professor, waving him away. "I'm just an old man, and my nerves are on edge after the trouble we've had today."

Mr. Spofford glanced quickly at the professor, and he seemed to be about to say something. But he changed his mind and turned instead to the clock.

"It's really somethin', ain't it?" he said, patting the side of the heavy wooden case. "By the way, professor.

You said you knew the guy who made this thing. Would you mind tellin' me about this M. Childermass? I'd kinda like t'know."

The professor straightened up and turned to face Mr. Spofford. "Very well," he said dryly. "If you're dying to know, I'll tell you. The clock was made by my father, Marcus Childermass, and it took him five years to do it. He began work on it shortly after my granduncle, Lucius J. Childermass, died. The doll is supposed to represent Uncle Lucius, who died in a very strange manner, and very suddenly, in this room—or rather, in the room of which this is a replica."

Johnny turned and stared in wonder at the professor. "You never told me anything about that," he said in a half-accusing tone.

The professor grimaced. "It's not a thing that I like to think about, or talk about. Uncle Lucius was found dead one snowy evening, on the day after Christmas. He was sitting in that black leather chair there, by the oval table. His head was thrown back and on his face was the most awful look of terror. Also—and this is the strangest part —those who examined the body found bits of foul-smelling earth in his mouth and on the front of his coat. Make something of *that*, if you can!"

"Boy, that is strange!" said Mr. Spofford, scratching his head. "Did they ever find out what the old—er, I mean, your granduncle—died of?"

The professor shook his head. "No, they did not. There was an inquest, and the coroner's verdict was 'Death by unknown causes.' It was what they used to call 'Death by the visitation of God.' And indeed, that is what a lot of people thought—that God had reached out and robbed Uncle Lucius of his life." The professor sighed. "I will add that that explanation was as good as any that people were able to come up with. No one was ever able to find any evidence of foul play."

Mr. Spofford looked thoughtful. He folded his arms on his chest and scowled, and then he threw a quick look at the clock. "And so your dad started to work on that clock there right after your uncle died? Did he mean it to be . . . like a memorial?"

"I suppose you might say that," muttered the professor. "Whatever the clock was supposed to be, it became an obsession with my father. He worked on it every chance he could get—but since he was a busy man, it took him a long time to finish the thing." The professor turned suddenly to Mr. Spofford and stared at him hard. "But tell me," he said, "what's all this business about the clock being haunted?"

Mr. Spofford acted startled, and then he looked a bit frightened. He laughed, but it was an unconvincing laugh—it sounded forced, and a bit hoarse. "Oh, *that*! Well, uh . . . well, that was just a *story*! You know how things get started. My wife, she had a funny dream about the clock an' . . . well, that's where that idea came from. Just one o' my wife's dumb notions, that's all!"

Mr. Spofford *heh-heh*'ed a bit and tried to act nonchalant, but he was not fooling the professor. He hated it when people tried to get evasive with him, and now his stare became fierce and hostile.

"Look!" he said angrily, jabbing his finger at Mr. Spofford. "You told me a few minutes ago that there were rumors of the clock being haunted. You seemed quite serious at the time, but now you're trying to make it all into a big fat joke. Would you mind leveling with me? I'm not three years old, you know, and I'd really like to find out the truth in this matter."

But Mr. Spofford would not say anything more, and so there was nothing left for the professor to do but say good night. Johnny shook Mr. Spofford's hand and thanked him, and then he and his elderly friend went upstairs to their nice warm beds.

Later that night Johnny was awakened from a deep sleep by a rattling sound. He sat up and shook his head groggily. What was making that noise? He glanced to his left and saw a window whitened by frost. Outside, the wind was blowing, and a bare branch was clattering and clawing against the window. The end of the branch was shaped a bit like a hand, and so it was easy for Johnny to imagine that it was some awful creature out there trying to get in. Johnny closed his eyes and shook his head. He tried to get rid of the unpleasant pictures that were forming in his mind. Then he opened his eyes again and stared out into the dark room. The professor was asleep in a bed over against the far wall. Johnny could hear the regular snortling sounds he was making. Noiselessly Johnny slipped out of bed and put on his slippers and bathrobe. He padded to the door, opened it, and stepped out into the hall. The hall was chilly and drafty. A dim night-light burned at the top of the stairs. With an odd, dreamy look on his face, Johnny gripped the railing and started down.

The downstairs hall was dark, and it was even colder than upstairs. Icy air slithered in through the crack at the bottom of the front door, and it stung Johnny's bare ankles. But he moved on, like a sleepwalker, to the door that led to the workroom where the Childermass clock was kept. He paused outside the dark door and put his hands on the wood paneling, listening. He heard sounds, voices. It was as if people were muttering excitedly inside the room. What were they saying? It was impossible to make it out. Johnny's hand moved toward the white china knob. He twisted it and pushed the door inward. Then he gasped.

CHAPTER TWO

Johnny was surrounded by darkness, not the darkness of a small room, but an immense well of blackness. It was as if he were standing in a great hall or a cathedral. Before him, like a window in the night, was a lighted room. It was small and seemed very far away, yet somehow he could see every detail. It was like the dollhouse room in the old clock, but it was a real room in a real house. It was night, and Johnny could see snow falling outside the window at the back of the room. The oil lamp on the table was lit, and a fire burned in the white marble fireplace.

The figure in the room was like the doll, but it was a living man, an old, distinguished-looking gentleman with a gray beard and rimless spectacles. He was pacing back and forth before the fire, and he looked worried. As Johnny watched, he sat down in the leather chair by the table, picked up the Bible, and began to leaf through it. Eventually he found a part that interested him, and he settled down to read. From far away Johnny heard the ghostly ticking of the mantel clock and the crackling of the fire. The old man read for a while and soon grew tired. He took off his glasses and slid them into the case on the table. After stifling a yawn, he rubbed his hands over his face. Then he leaned his head back, folded his hands in his lap, and dozed off. Johnny watched, wide-eyed. Blood roared in his ears, and his fists were clenched, but he stayed rooted to the spot: what would happen next?

He didn't have long to wait. As the old man slept, a subtle change came over the room. The flame of the oil lamp grew dim and dwindled to a blue point. The fire in the fireplace died, as if some unseen force were smothering it. And then a door in the rear wall of the room began to open. The light that fell through the doorway was cold, pale, and wavering. At first Johnny saw only the open door and the watery, shimmering light. Then he saw a tall, gaunt shadow that moved with dragging steps through the doorway and into the room. The light was poor, and so Johnny could not tell much about the shape, except that it was fearfully thin and appeared to be wearing ragged clothes. As he watched, the shape moved toward the sleeping man and hovered over him. The old man opened his eyes and looked up, and Johnny heard him scream. It was a thin wailing sound that seemed to come from far away, and it chilled Johnny to the bone. The old man shrank back in his chair as the gaunt, menacing figure bent over him. It stretched out a long thin hand and covered the old man's face, and then the old man began to struggle and writhe. Frantically he tried to push the hand away, but his struggles got weaker and weaker, and finally he lay still, slumped back in the chair. A pause. Then the figure took its hand away from the old man's face, bent over, and peered horribly close, as if it were trying to make sure that the man was really dead. Finally the shadowy form straightened up, shuffled toward the door, and went out. Immediately the scene went black. And Johnny was left alone in the dark cold workroom, listening to the wind that keened and moaned around the corners of the ancient inn.

For a long time Johnny cowered in the dark, wide-eyed and wondering. He was awed and frightened by what he had seen. But what was it that he had witnessed? It looked like the murder of Professor Childermass's granduncle. If that was it, then who had the murderer been? Was it a ghost who had snuffed out the life of the old man? And finally Johnny asked himself this question: Why had he, John Dixon, been brought down here to see this strange, ghostly drama? Was he supposed to warn the professor about something? And if so, what? Johnny had no answers for any of these questions. As he peered nervously around in the dark, he saw the faint outline of the old clock looming on the table next to the workbench. Shuddering, he turned and felt his way to the door. But the room was very dark, and as Johnny groped along, he caught his toe on the end of a loose floorboard and lurched up against the table that held the Childermass clock. From inside the clock came a jangling of chimes and a rattle of machinery, and then —to his horror—Johnny heard something roll out across the tabletop and drop onto the floor. It sounded like something small, maybe one of the delicate pieces of furniture from the dollhouse room.

Filled with guilt and worry, and already making up apologies in his mind, Johnny dropped to his knees and began scrabbling around on the floor with his hands. His fingers closed over something small and round, like a marble. Pulling himself to his feet, Johnny took a step toward the dark clock. But shouldn't he switch the light on so he could see what he was doing? Turning, Johnny took a few stumbling steps toward the door. Then— strangely—instead of trying to find the light switch, he grasped the doorknob, opened the door, and stepped out into the hall.

With the door closed behind him, Johnny leaned against the wall, breathing heavily, and opened his hand. The light out here in the hall was dim, but he could see what he had—the skull! With an odd, fasci-nated expression on his face, Johnny turned the grotesque little object over in his hand. Then, with a sudden motion, he shoved the skull into his bathrobe pocket and padded on down the hall.

Johnny did not get any more sleep that night. He went back up to bed, but he tossed and turned and kept glancing nervously at the door of his bedroom. If it had suddenly begun to open, he was sure that he would have gone out of his mind with fear. But the door stayed shut, and Johnny lay there fretting and listening to the wind. He thought about what he had seen and about the tiny, toylike skull that he had stolen. It was in the pocket of his corduroy pants now, where he had stuffed it for safe-keeping. Why didn't he want to give it back? Johnny couldn't say, but he did know one thing: when dawn came, he was very glad to see it.

Later that morning Johnny and the professor were down in the dining room of the inn having a wonderful wintertime breakfast, pancakes and sausage and hot coffee, but Johnny was not eating much of it. He felt totally socked. There were dark circles around his eyes, and his face felt prickly.

"John," the professor said anxiously, "you really look *terrible* this morning! What on earth is the matter? Did my snoring keep you awake?"

Johnny put down the piece of sausage that he was toying with and glanced warily at the professor. He realized that he ought to tell his friend what had happened last night. It was a strange and unlikely tale, but he was sure the professor would believe him. And it would get an incredible load off his chest. Nervously Johnny stuck his right hand into his pants pocket. His fingers twiddled with the ivory skull, and he opened his mouth to speak—but something unexpected happened. He found that he couldn't talk! His jaw shuddered, and he struggled, but nothing came out. There was a pain in his chest, as if a band of steel were wrapped around his body, and someone were twisting it tighter. Finally Johnny stopped trying. He slumped back in his chair, exhausted. Sweat was streaming down his face, and he was scared half out of his mind.

The professor was stunned. "My Lord, John!" he exclaimed. "What in heaven's name is the matter? I've never seen you like this before! Do you want me to call a doctor? What should I do?"

Johnny didn't know what to say—he didn't even know if he *could* say anything. But the pain in his chest had gone, and he was breathing more easily. He was feeling better because he had stopped trying to tell the professor about the vision he had seen. Frightened, Johnny knew that he had to yield to this spell—or whatever it was—that had been cast on him.

"I . . . I guess it was just heart-heartburn or something like that," he muttered faintly. He closed his eyes, took out his handkerchief, and mopped his forehead. "I . . . I'm sorry I scared you," he added.

The professor was still quite concerned. He had seen cases of food poisoning when he was in the army, and he knew it could be fatal. He was ready to go out to the kitchen and give the cook a severe talking-to, but Johnny insisted that he was okay. And so the two of them went back to eating.

After an uncomfortable silence Johnny spoke up again. "How's your car doing?" he asked. "Is . . . is it wrecked, or can we go home in it?"

The professor made a sour face. "Ah, yes, my car! Well, I went over to Finsterwald's Garage before breakfast, and they told me that I could stagger on home with it. They said I might get picked up for having only one headlight, but considering all the one-eyed cars I've seen driving around in the last year, I will be *very* put out if the cops stop me. Yes, it's driveable . . . but the bill for the towing and the etcetera is not pretty, it's not pretty at all! However, I suppose it must be paid. . . ." The professor's voice trailed off. He leaned forward and stared hard at Johnny. "Are you *sure* you're okay? You're in my care while we're on this trip, and I'd feel awful if something happened to you. Please be honest with me. If you're feeling ill, I'll take you to a doctor and have you checked up."

Johnny really got flustered this time. He did not want to be taken anywhere for a checkup. So he gritted his teeth, smiled in what he hoped was a reassuring way, and forced himself to eat two mouthfuls of pancakes and syrup. "Yeah, I'm all right," he mumbled, as he chewed. "Let's not talk about it anymore, okay?"

After they had finished their meal, the professor went out to the front desk to settle the bill and Johnny went upstairs to the bedroom to get the suitcases. Then the two of them got ready to stump off through the snow to Finsterwald's Garage to fetch the poor battered Pontiac so they could drive home.

A month passed. The snow melted, and the ice on the Merrimack River broke up and washed out to sea. As the March winds boomed in the trees, kids started playing softball on muddy vacant lots. Johnny Dixon went on with his usual life. He did homework, watched television, and went places with his best friend, Fergie. He helped his grandfather carry out the ashes from the furnace and raked up some soggy leaves that were left from last fall. He visited with the professor and ate pieces of his delicious cakes and played chess and backgammon with him. But all the while, in the back of his mind, he carried around the memory of the eerie scene that had been played before his eyes in that dark back room in the Fitzwilliam Inn. Several times he got his courage up and decided that he would try to tell the professor about what had happened. But each time he felt that awful tightening pain in the chest and a deep nameless fear that was enough to stop him. Of course, he could have tried to tell somebody else about his experience, but in his mind the whole incident was surrounded with fear. It was as if he had done something horrible that he didn't dare talk about. So Johnny just kept quiet about that cold windy February night. He didn't tell Grampa or Gramma or Fergie or anybody.

He also kept clammed up about the skull. It was funny how he felt about it: He wanted to protect the thing, to preserve it from harm. For a while he carried it in his pocket, but he got worried that it would drop out through a hole in his pants or get scarred up by coins or his house keys. So he put the skull in an old blue watchcase with a snap lid, and he kept it hidden under the shirts in his top bureau drawer. Now and then his conscience would prick him, and he would feel guilty about keeping the skull. Shouldn't he wrap it up and send it back to the Fitzwilliam Inn? He could do it anonymously and stay out of trouble that way. But then he told himself that skulls were lucky. He remembered the story the professor had told him about Mexican village festivals, where they made candy skulls and ate them for good luck. And now that he thought about it, it was possible that the skull had saved him from an awful fate. He remembered the shadowy evil shape he had seen in the vision. What if it had decided to go after him? It might have done just that if the skull had not fallen out of the dollhouse room and landed at his feet. Perhaps there was some kindly force at work in the haunted clock, a force that had said, *Here, take this talisman—it will protect you from harm.* This was the way Johnny reasoned, and his reasoning always led him to one conclusion—he'd better hang on to the skull and keep it safe.

On a Thursday night late in the month of March, Johnny and his friend Fergie were doing their homework in the parlor of the Dixon house. They went to different schools, in different parts of the city, but they both were taking Latin, and right now they were helping each other memorize the demonstrative pronoun *hic, haec, hoc*. *Hic, haec, hoc* just means *this*, but it has lots of forms, and you have to memorize them if you are going to pass beginning Latin. Fergie was a gangly, skinny kid with dark skin, black, greasy, curly hair, a long, blunt-ended nose, enormous ears, and droopy features. At this moment he was trying to get through *hic, haec, hoc* without a mistake.

"*Hic, haec, hoc,*" Fergie began, "*hujus, hupus, hujus; huic, huic, huic; hunc, hanc, hoc . . .*" Fergie's voice began to waver—he was getting the giggles, as he always did when he said these silly words too many times. He fought the laughter down and struggled on: "*Hoc, hac, hoc. Hi, hae, haec; horum, harum . . .*" But it was no use—he couldn't go on. He was giggling helplessly now.

Usually when this kind of thing happened, Johnny would break into laughter too. But this time he got angry. His face turned red, and he slammed the book shut. "Oh, come *on*, Fergie!" he yelled. "Will you cut that out! We've got *work* to do!"

Fergie was so startled by Johnny's outburst that he stopped giggling. He stared, open-mouthed. What on earth was the matter with his friend?

"Hey," he said in a soft, wondering tone, "what's got into you, John baby? I mean, it's not all *that* important, to lose your temper about! It's just a crummy Latin test, and you'll probably cream it anyway—you always do. So why're you in such an uproar, huh?"

Johnny put down the book he was holding. He wiped his hand across his face and shook his head. Sometimes you can be in a rotten mood and not know it until you pop off at somebody. That was the way it was with Johnny today. And it wasn't just bad temper all by itself. He had had a deep sense of foreboding all day. In his belly he felt that something bad was going to happen to somebody that he knew. He had brooded and worried, and that was why he was so edgy right now. He felt like somebody who is waiting for a thunderstorm to break loose on the world.

"I . . . I'm sorry, Fergie, honest I am," he stammered. "I dunno what's the matter with me. I've been worried all day about . . . about something. I keep thinking that a really awful thing is gonna happen."

"You mean, like you might step on a nail and get tetanus?" said Fergie, grinning. He knew about Johnny's fear of tetanus, and it amused him no end.

Johnny shook his head. "Nope," he said miserably. "It's not something that's gonna happen to me. It's gonna happen to somebody I know, like you or Gramma or Grampa or the professor. I don't know why I have this darned feeling. I just do, that's all."

Fergie frowned skeptically. He was a real no-nonsense type—at least he tried to be. In some ways he was just as superstitious as Johnny, but he put up a good front. He was always saying that he believed in science and cold, hard facts. "You're probably just comin' down with a cold," he said, shrugging. "My uncle Harvey always used to think that he was gonna die durin' the night, while he was sleepin'. But he didn't—he got killed in a car crash. You can't believe in these funny feelings that you get."

"Maybe not," said Johnny. He grimaced and bit his lip. "All the same," he went on, "I wish I knew why I felt this . . ."

Johnny's voice died. He had been looking around while he talked, and he had happened to peer out the big bay window. Across the street was the professor's house, an enormous two-story barn of a place. There were lights on downstairs, but the upstairs windows were dark. Except for one. In it an orange jack-o'-lantern face glowed.

Johnny was utterly astonished. "Hey!" he exclaimed, poking Fergie in the arm. "Look at that, would you!"

Fergie looked, and he did a double take. Then he let out a long, low whistle. "Wow!" he said, shaking his head in awe. "Your pal the professor has finally gone out of his jug! I mean, he's only about seven months early for Halloween! My gosh! Whaddaya think of that?"

Johnny didn't know what to think. But his sense of foreboding came back, stronger than ever. It was true that the professor had a weird sense of humor, but making a jack-o'-lantern in March . . . well, it just didn't seem like the kind of thing he would do. For a long time Johnny just stood there, watching, while the grinning orange mask hovered in the darkness. Then—reluctantly —he went back to working on his Latin with Fergie.

Johnny thought a lot about the jack-o'-lantern that evening. After Fergie had gone home, he wondered if maybe he ought to call the professor up and see if everything was all right. Which—as Johnny told himself— was a silly, worrywart kind of thought. Why *shouldn't* everything be all right? If the professor wanted to make jack-o'-lanterns in March, that was his business. And it probably didn't mean that he had gone out of his mind, or was going to hang himself from the chandelier in the dining room. The professor was an oddball, and oddballs did peculiar, unpredictable things. And yet . . . there were still a lot of *and yet*'s in Johnny's anxious mind when he went to bed that night.

The next morning, as Johnny was leaving the house to go to school, he saw the professor backing his car out of his driveway. Probably he was heading for Haggstrum College, where he taught history. Suddenly a thought seized Johnny: He ought to go over and make some mention of the jack-o'-lantern to the professor, just to see what his reaction would be. Quickly he ran down the steps and out into the street. He was waiting as the professor's car slid slowly past, spewing clouds of exhaust smoke. Johnny reached out and rapped on the car window with his knuckles, so the professor would know he was there. The car halted, and the window rolled down. As soon as the professor saw that it was Johnny, he grinned.

"Good morning, John!" he said, smiling wearily. "As you see, I'm on my way to that wonderful temple of learning where I try to beat ideas into the heads of dullards. Would you care for a ride to school?"

Johnny said that yes, he'd like a ride. But there was something he wanted to ask the professor about first.

"Oh, really?" said the professor dryly. "Would you like to know about torture methods in sixteenth-century England? Or how many blows of the axe it took to chop off the Duke of Monmouth's head? Something like that?"

Johnny laughed. "Nope. I just wanta know how come you made a jack-o'-lantern when it's only March."

The professor's mouth dropped open. He was utterly dumbfounded. "You want to know how come I made a *what?*"

Now it was Johnny's turn to be astonished. This was not a reply that he had expected. Of course, the professor might be kidding—but he didn't act it. "I . . . I mean the j-jack-o'-lantern that w-was in your up-upstairs window last n-night," said Johnny. He often stammered when he was flustered or upset.

The professor continued to stare at Johnny. "My dear friend," he said slowly and gravely, "either this is some kind of bizarre joke that you're trying out on me, or you need to get a new pair of glasses! I don't make jack-o'-lanterns even when it *is* Halloween! They attract trick-or-treaters, and I cannot stand that kind of silly, greedy rigmarole! John, honestly, I have no idea of what you're talking about. Are you sure you didn't see the reflection of the moon? Or maybe it was my bedside lamp. It has a reddish shade. Well, if you don't mind, I think we'd better be getting on, or we'll both be late for school. Hop in, won't you?"

Johnny opened and shut his mouth a couple of times, but he couldn't think of anything to say. He sighed weakly, walked around the car, and climbed in. As they drove down the street he sat staring numbly at the dashboard. He felt dazed. Was he going out of his mind? No, that couldn't be, because Fergie had seen the jack-o'-lantern too. With a sick feeling he realized that there was another possible explanation: The professor might be losing *his* mind. Johnny had heard that sometimes old people got very scatty and did peculiar things, and even forgot the names and faces of people they had known all their lives. But the professor did not act like someone who had lost his marbles—he was behaving just like his usual cranky but likeable self. It was all very strange. Again Johnny had the urge to tell the professor about the vision—or dream, or whatever it was—that he had seen at the Fitzwilliam Inn. He opened his mouth to speak, but suddenly he felt that shortness of breath, that tightening in the chest. And he decided that he had better think of other things until it was time to get out of the car.

That evening, after school, Johnny and Fergie went to the movies together. This was a Friday-night habit of theirs, and they went in good weather or bad, to lousy movies or to good ones. On this particular Friday, they happened to land a really rousing, slam-bang pirate movie. They always sat way down in front and munched popcorn and made smart remarks, until the usher came down and threatened to throw them out if they didn't shut up. After the show, as they walked the dark, windy streets, Fergie and Johnny talked about the professor and the problem of the jack-o'-lantern that was—or was not—there.

". . . and he claimed that he never made one, and he got really huffy and acted insulted when I said he did," Johnny was saying as they stood at a corner, waiting for the light to change. "But you saw it, didn't you?"

"Yeah . . . I guess so," said Fergie uncertainly. He wrinkled up his nose, as if he were smelling something unpleasant. Fergie liked mysteries, but he always felt they ought to have nice, reasonable explanations. "Sure —there was a jack-o'-lantern," he added as the light changed and they started across the street. "An' I'll tell you how come the old so-and-so made it: He got a little schnockered an' he carved it out, jist fer fun, an' then when you asked him about it, he got embarrassed an' tried to lie his way out. How's that for an answer to your great big fat mystery? Huh?"

Johnny gave Fergie a dirty look. He liked the professor a lot, and he didn't enjoy hearing anybody call him an "old so-and-so." Also, to tell the truth, he did not think much of Fergie's wonderful explanation.

"The professor doesn't ever get drunk," said Johnny, frowning stubbornly. "And besides, when I asked him about the jack-o'-lantern, he didn't act embarrassed—he really didn't! He just looked at me like I was from outer space. Like he'd never heard anything so unbelievable in his life."

Fergie stooped and picked up a rock that lay on the sidewalk. He threw it across the street, and it pinged loudly as it bounced off a fire hydrant. "Maybe he's a real good actor," said Fergie, who could be just as stubborn as Johnny when he thought he was right.

"He's not *that* good an actor," muttered Johnny, digging his hands deep into the pockets of his jacket.

"Well, then, what the heck *was* the darned thing?" exclaimed Fergie impatiently. "Was it a mirage, like the kind they have out in the desert? It had to be real—it just *had* to be! And don't tell me it was a ghost. That's the next thing you'll be tryin' to say!"

Silence fell. The two boys trudged moodily along, staring at the sidewalk. Two blocks passed, and then they reached the Main Street Bridge. Fergie lived over in Cranbrook, on the other side of the bridge.

Fergie threw a shamefaced glance at Johnny. He wanted to stay friends, and he was beginning to be afraid that he had hurt Johnny's feelings by telling him that his ideas were dumb.

"Look," said Fergie hurriedly, "I gotta go. But we can talk about this later. Maybe we can figure out what really happened."

"Yeah, maybe," muttered Johnny. He wanted to be alone, so he could think things out. "See ya around."

Fergie turned and walked off into the darkness. Johnny trotted across Main Street and started climbing the steep hill toward home. The wind had let up, and the night was still. Up ahead, off to the right, loomed the dark shadow of the professor's house. Johnny glanced up, and his jaw dropped. There, leering down at him from a second-story window, was the jack-o'-lantern.

Fear clutched at Johnny's heart. He told himself that he was being silly, that this was the professor's idea of a joke. For a long time Johnny just stood there, gazing like a hypnotized person at the sinister, grinning mask. Then, abruptly, he made a decision: he had to find out what was going on. Johnny raced across the street and cut through a gap in the spirea hedge that bordered the professor's front yard. Nervously he scanned the front of the house. Overhead the lantern burned, but the downstairs windows were dark. He could see that the window over the porch was lit—that was the professor's study, where he often was at this time of night.

Warily Johnny crept forward. Acorns and twigs crunched under his feet, and he stumbled over a dead limb. But he righted himself and moved steadily on. He could see that the back porch light was on, and there was a lamp lit in the kitchen too. Johnny paused. *Why was he so tense?* Blood was pounding in his temples, and he kept expecting to see horrible things come rushing at him out of nowhere. But nothing happened, and he edged closer to the back porch. He tried the screen door.

It was unlocked. So was the inside door. The professor's kitchen was in its usual messy state, with unwashed dishes piled in the sink. A saucepan with something black burned inside it was sitting on the stove, and the kitchen table was covered with flour. An old-fashioned Waterbury clock ticked quietly on a shelf above the spice rack.

"Hello!" Johnny called, cupping his hands to his mouth. "Professor? Are you home?"

No answer. Johnny felt embarrassed. He shouldn't be barging in on his old friend this way. But he just *had* to find out about that lantern. Also, for no reason that he could put his finger on, there was a growing fear that something bad might have happened to Professor Childermass.

Johnny walked through the first floor of the house, peering into empty rooms and calling the professor's name. At the bottom of the stairs he paused again. Should he go up? Maybe the professor was just out for an evening stroll. He might come back at any minute. Or he might be upstairs in his study, correcting papers or reading. Johnny gritted his teeth.

One more try first. Cupping his hands, Johnny bellowed up the stairs: *"Hey, professor! Are you home?"*

Again no answer. Clenching his fists resolutely, Johnny strode up the steps. At the top he paused a second longer and then headed for the professor's study. The door was ajar, and the desk lamp was on. Everything looked perfectly normal. The professor's desk was littered with blue examination books, and the stuffed owl on the pillar in the corner glowered indignantly at Johnny. But the desk chair was empty. As Johnny moved farther into the room, he saw some things that astonished and disturbed him. On the desk pad, next to the pile of exam books, was a cup of coffee. Steam curled up from it—it was still hot! And, perched on the lip of the glass ashtray, was one of the professor's black-and-gold Balkan Sobranie cigarettes. It was half-smoked and still lit. The pungent aroma of the cigarette tickled Johnny's nostrils. Had the professor been called out of the room a second or two ago? If so, where was he?

Johnny went out into the hall. He glanced toward the bathroom. But the door was open, and from where he was standing he could see that the room was dark. He was really panicky now—he could feel his palms sweating. He crept to the entrance of the professor's bedroom and, with a sudden motion, flung the door inward. It banged loudly against the wall, and the violent noise almost made Johnny scream. But he got control of himself and flipped on the overhead light: nobody there. Johnny braced himself for the next step. He had to go down to the room where the jack-o'-lantern was. Nervously he clenched and unclenched his fists and tried to calm himself. *Why was he so scared to do this?* With a grim frown on his face, he strode boldly down the hall and stopped outside the massive paneled oak door. With a loud exclamation he seized the knob and twisted it. The door flew open, and Johnny's hand fumbled for the light switch. A harsh glare flooded the room. In it was a gloomy mahogany bed, a marble-topped bureau, and a chair with a caned seat. White lace curtains hung on the room's only window. There was no jack-o'-lantern. There wasn't even a table or stand on which one could have been standing. Nor was there the smell of hot pumpkin and candle wax that hung in the air where a jack-o'-lantern had been burning. The only smell in the room was the wonderful aroma of balsam-fir needles that rose from a pillow-shaped white packet that lay on top of the bureau. A canoeing scene was picked out in green thread on the surface of the cloth packet, along with the words WELCOME TO NEW HAMPSHIRE.

Johnny fought down the shapeless fear that was in his mind. At the far end of the narrow room, next to the window, was a closet door. Could there be a jack-o'-lantern in there? Maybe one of those new plastic ones, with a light bulb in it. That would explain why . . .

Halfway to the window Johnny froze. He had seen something out of the corner of his eye, a sudden image in the small rectangular mirror that hung over the bureau. He turned and looked. In the mirror he saw the professor's face, looking haggard and disheveled. His eyes pleaded and, as Johnny watched, his lips formed silent words. "*Help me.*"

CHAPTER THREE

Johnny gazed, horror-struck. As he watched, the picture in the mirror dissolved into writhing curls of steam. The steam evaporated, and Johnny was looking at his own frightened face. Somehow, he got out of the room. He galloped down the hall, down the stairs, and out the back door, slamming it hard behind him. Outside, under the cold stars again, he halted. His face was streaming with sweat, and he was breathing hard. *"What can I do, what can I do, what . . ."* Johnny babbled hysterically. Then he pulled himself together. There was nothing he could do—not right away. Something awful, something supernatural, had happened to the professor. But at least he was alive. If he weren't, he would not have been able to speak to Johnny from the mirror. But where was he? In outer space? In another dimension? Buried deep under the earth? Where? And what did his disappearance have to do with the ghostly scene that Johnny had seen in the Fitzwilliam Inn? Johnny had no answer to any of these questions. He was totally, thoroughly stumped.

Suddenly Johnny realized that he was supposed to be home. His grandmother always worried about him when he was out at night. By now she would be phoning all the—

A sound interrupted Johnny's thoughts. It was a phone ringing inside the professor's house. He knew who that was. Throwing a quick glance at the silent, empty house, he set out for home on the run.

Gramma was waiting for him on the front steps. The porch light was on, and he could see plainly that she was not in a good mood. Gramma was frowning darkly, and her arms were folded across the front of her apron.

"John Dixon," she said angrily, "what on *earth* do you mean by stayin' out so late? I've been worried sick about you! I called the movie theater, an'—"

"Gramma," said Johnny, cutting in on her excitedly, "there . . . there's something wrong across the street. The professor's gone! He's disappeared!"

Gramma snorted skeptically. "Huh! I'll just bet he has! Young man, is that the best excuse you c'n come up with? Eh?"

Johnny's heart sank. He felt utterly helpless. How was he ever going to explain to his grandmother what he had seen? Gramma was superstitious, but she would hardly believe what he had to tell her. What would she say if he started talking about phantom jack-o'-lanterns and ghostly faces in mirrors?

Johnny hung his head and looked ashamed. "I . . . I'm sorry I stayed out late," he said in a low, hesitant voice. "I forgot what time it was and . . . and I had a question about my schoolwork that I wanted to ask the professor. I won't do it again. Please don't be angry."

Gramma's harsh look softened, and she smiled and opened the screen door for Johnny. "All right, young man," she said, trying hard to sound stern and forbidding, "but don't let this kind of behavior turn into a habit. You run on upstairs 'n' brush your teeth 'n' wash your face 'n' get off to bed! It's gonna be rise 'n' shine early tomorrow mornin', so you better catch some shuteye."

"He really is gone, Gramma," said Johnny, glancing quickly at the old woman. "The professor, I mean—he's not there!"

Gramma shrugged. "Old bachelors like him keep funny kinds of hours," she said as she hooked the screen. "If you're all by yourself you c'n stay up all night 'n' nobody'll mind. But don't you worry. He'll be comin' outa that front door in the early A.M., just like he always does."

Johnny shook his head gloomily. After what he had seen, he knew very well that the professor was not going to be there tomorrow. Or the next day, or the day after that. Johnny felt horribly frustrated. He wanted to yell that she was wrong. He wanted to tell her that witchcraft and dark mysterious forces were involved in the professor's disappearance. But with a mighty effort, he forced his feelings back down inside. Grimly he plodded up the stairs. He went to his room and put on his pajamas. After brushing his teeth he flung himself into bed and lay there, wide-eyed, waiting for the sleep that he knew was not going to come.

All that night Johnny tossed and turned. Again and again the professor's tormented face appeared before him. *Help me. Help me.* And Johnny wanted to scream back at him, *How? How'm I gonna help you, I don't even know where you are!* Twice he jumped out of bed and ran to the window to stare wildly at the professor's house. He kept hoping that he would see his old friend come ambling up the walk. But the street lamp threw its cold light on the empty sidewalk, and the professor's house stayed dark. Back in bed again, Johnny tried a new angle: Had he been hallucinating? The mind could play tricks—he knew that. But he was so utterly sure that he had seen the face in the mirror. And then there was the jack-o'-lantern—Fergie had seen it too. And on top of everything else, Johnny still had the nagging feeling that the vision he had seen in the Fitzwilliam Inn—the vision that he couldn't tell the professor about—had something to do with this mystery. Some evil force had kept him from telling the professor about the ghostly scene he had witnessed. Why? If the professor had known about the vision, would he have guessed about what was going to happen to him? Nothing made any sense to Johnny at this point. In his mind he feverishly chased old clocks and inns and grinning jack-o'-lanterns around and around and around. When dawn came, he felt exhausted, as if he had been running for miles. He also felt heartsick: He knew his dear old friend was gone, and he wondered if he would ever see him again.

In the morning Johnny was so socked that he hardly knew what he was doing. He clumped down the front staircase slowly, as if there were weights on his feet. When he reached the bottom, he saw the front door was open. Grampa was standing out on the porch, taking in the morning air. He was a tall, stooped, friendly old man in his midseventies, and he wore gray work shirts and gray wash pants all the time. Instead of heading out to the kitchen for breakfast, Johnny decided that he would go out and talk to Grampa for a minute. And he was desperately hoping that he would see the professor come out of his house as usual, get into his car, and drive off to the college to teach his Saturday-morning World History class.

Grampa turned as he heard the porch boards creak behind him. "Oh, hi, Johnny!" he said with a little wave of his hand. "Nice mornin', huh?"

"Uh huh," said Johnny, and he forced himself to smile. He stepped out onto the front stoop and stood next to Grampa. Putting his hands in his pockets, he tried to act casual. But he wasn't really nonchalant—he was terribly interested in seeing signs of life across the street. Straining his eyes, he tried to see through the dingy windows of the professor's garage door. But it was impossible for him to tell if the old beat-up Pontiac was in or out.

"Has the professor left yet?" he asked in a tense voice.

Grampa frowned and shook his head. "Nope. He might be sick t'day, er else maybe he finally got rid o' that Saturday class of his. Funny though . . . most o' the time he's up an' out by now."

Again Johnny experienced that sick feeling rising inside him. He felt totally helpless. He wanted to drag Grampa across the street and make him search the professor's house. But what good would that do? Johnny felt uncontrollable tears welling up inside him. Abruptly he turned and ran inside, and Grampa watched him go with a wondering frown on his face.

Somehow Johnny got through breakfast. Then an idea hit him. He would call up Fergie and get him to meet him. Skeptic or no skeptic, Fergie was his best friend. He was going to have to listen to his story.

"Hello? Ferguson residence. Byron speaking." Fergie sounded grumpy, but then he always did in the morning. Johnny had been to Boy Scout camp with Fergie, and he knew he was the slowest waker-upper in the world.

"Hi. It's me, John. Can I talk to you a minute?"

"Yeah, I guess so. I was just on my way out the door. So what's up?"

"I want you to meet me down at Peter's Sweet Shop right away. I've got something I have to talk to you about."

Fergie snickered. "What is it? You gettin' married? You want my advice about your love life?"

Now Johnny felt irritated. Fergie knew that he was shy with girls, and he liked to kid him about it. "No, it isn't that, lover boy. So can you meet me or not?"

"Yeah, sure, I'll meet you," said Fergie amiably. "See ya later." And he hung up.

Peter's Sweet Shop was an old-fashioned soda fountain with a marble counter and high stools and deep wooden booths with curly sides. There were colored glass lamps, and a jukebox, plus a display case up in front with boxes of candy in it. The kids of Duston Heights came to Peter's all the time after school and on weekends to eat hot fudge sundaes and slurp sodas and other gooey treats. As soon as he could get away from the house, Johnny headed straight down there. When he arrived, he found Fergie perched on a stool, drinking a cherry Coke.

"Hi, Dixon!" he said, smiling sarcastically. "So what's the big deal? Government secrets? Are you a Commie, and you wanta confess to me?"

Johnny frowned. He was not in a mood for kidding. "C'mon," he muttered, motioning toward the back of the store. "Let's get a booth, an' then I'll tell you the whole deal."

Fergie followed Johnny to the back of the shop. They

slid into one of the booths, and a waitress came over and asked for their order. Fergie ordered a dish of fudge ripple ice cream to go with his Coke, and Johnny asked for a chocolate frappe. The waitress went away, and Johnny eyed Fergie nervously. How was he going to manage to tell him this strange, unlikely tale?

"Well?" said Fergie, grinning expectantly.

Johnny squirmed in his seat. He folded and unfolded his hands and stared hard at the Formica tabletop. "Look," he began slowly, "you . . . you remember that jack-o'-lantern we were talkin' about?"

Fergie groaned and covered his face with his hand. "Oh, *no!* Dixon, come *off* it! Not that jack-o'-lantern business again! Can't you just—"

"*No, I can't! This is serious business, Fergie, so just be quiet and listen, or else leave!*" Color had flooded into Johnny's face, and he looked wild.

Fergie was startled. Most of the time Johnny was a mild-mannered, timid kid. This outburst caught Fergie off guard—now he was the one who felt shy and nervous.

"Okay, okay!" said Fergie softly. "Don't have a fit! Just tell me what it is you wanta tell me!"

So Johnny told about seeing the jack-o'-lantern again and about what he had found when he entered the professor's dark, silent house. He didn't leave anything out, and as he plunged headlong through this tale, he kept thinking: *I don't care if he thinks I'm crazy! I've GOTTA tell him!* Finally he was done. He sat back, tense and expectant. What would Fergie say?

At first Fergie was silent. Though he never would have admitted it, tales of the supernatural fascinated him. On the other hand he wasn't going to swallow every wild tale that his friend threw at him. He wanted some kind of proof before he accepted anything.

Fergie folded his hands and cracked his knuckles. He gazed out the window and tried to act skeptical and calm.

"Look, Dixon," he said quietly, "you don't wanta go flyin' off the handle. I mean, you might've seen somethin', but on the other hand you might've got panicky and *imagined* that you saw somethin'. No offense meant, but I think that's possible."

Johnny glared at Fergie. "I didn't imagine anything, and I saw what I saw! Now, are you gonna help me, or not?"

Fergie threw Johnny a quick, frightened glance. He had never seen Johnny act quite so forceful and downright certain before. This helped to convince Fergie that Johnny's tale might possibly be true.

"Oh, *okay*!" said Fergie, slamming his hand down hard on the table. "I feel like a dope, but I guess I hafta help you. Whaddaya think we oughta do?"

This question took Johnny by surprise. He really didn't have a plan of any kind. "I dunno," he said sheepishly. "I thought you might have some kind of an idea."

Fergie grinned. "Whaddaya think, I look like Sherlock Holmes er somethin'?" Seeing that Johnny was not amused, Fergie grew serious again. He drummed his fingers on the tabletop and stared hard at the melting ice cream in front of him. "Okay," he said wearily, "here's what I think: If the prof's really gone off into Dimension X or out to Mars, we aren't gonna get him back in a hurry. I mean, are we?"

Johnny shook his head glumly. "Nope," he said.

"*But!*" said Fergie, stabbing a forefinger at Johnny. "But still, and even if, he might be somewheres right on this earth, mightn't he?"

Johnny nodded.

"Right!" said Fergie. His eyes shone, and he acted agitated, as he always did when he was putting a logical train of thought together. "Okay then. We hafta find out where he is. And even if he's off with the mullygrubs on another planet, maybe we can figure out some way to bring him back. I mean, it's possible—*anything's* possible! But we need some clues. We hafta have something to go on! I think we oughta go back to his house an' snoop around. An' we better do it in a hurry. Pretty soon they're gonna know that the old guy really *is* missin'! I mean, your grampa and gramma and Mrs. Kovacs and the cops are gonna know, and they're all gonna be in the house pokin' around an' knockin' things over an' takin' things an' labelin' 'em Exhibit A an' so on. So we better get ourselves in gear an' hike on back to his place. Sound like a good idea to you?"

Johnny agreed. He took a few more slurps of his frappe, and Fergie gobbled some ice cream quickly. Then they paid their bill and headed out the door. Just as they were turning onto Fillmore Street they saw a police car parked out in front of the professor's house. Apparently the professor had missed his morning class, and someone from the college had driven out to his place to check up on him. The front door of the gray stucco mansion was open, and a small crowd of people had gathered on the sidewalk that led to the front porch. Johnny recognized Gramma and Grampa and Mr. Swartout and a few of the other neighbors. A short burly policeman with bushy gray hair was asking questions and jotting things down on a notepad. Another one was standing in front of the house with his arms folded, as if he were guarding the place.

Johnny's hand flew to his mouth, and his heart sank. "Oh, no!" he groaned. "How are we ever gonna get inside *now*?"

Fergie was not upset, however. "Come on, Dixon!" he snapped. "Use your old bean! We can just double back an' go down the alley that runs behind the garages an' then zip in the back door an' have ourselves a look around. Simple, eh?"

Johnny thought a second. He knew the alley, of course. He had used it many times to get to the other end of Fillmore Street without his grandmother seeing him. "Yeah, but wait a minute!" he said. "What if there's cops inside the house? What d'we do then?"

Fergie smiled cynically. "We just say 'Oops, sorry!' an' then skedaddle! You an' the prof are old friends. You can just say you left one o' your schoolbooks in his house.

It's not anything to get all that worked up about."

So Johnny and Fergie turned around and went back through the narrow alley that ran behind the houses on Fillmore Street. The yard gate next to the professor's garage was open. When they tried the back door, they found that it was locked, but Johnny knew that the spare key was kept under a flowerpot on the ledge of the kitchen window. Soon they were inside.

The kitchen was exactly as Johnny had seen it last night—nothing had been touched. Silently Fergie and Johnny crept through the big old house. Johnny led the way, telling Fergie that he wanted to check out the professor's study again. Last night he had been in such a panic that he hadn't really had a chance to observe much. And he was convinced that if the professor had left a farewell note or anything of that sort, it would be in the study.

The study door creaked as Johnny pushed it open. Everything looked just as it had last night: there on the desk were the scattered exam books, the cup of coffee (now cold), and the half-smoked cigarette in the ashtray.

"Wow! This place's a mess, isn't it?" whispered Fergie.

"Yeah, it usually is!" Johnny whispered back. He looked around. Yes, the professor's study was in its usual slovenly condition. Books were stuck any-which-way into the sagging bricks-and-boards bookcases. A dune of papers and looseleaf notebooks was heaped against the front of the big kneehole desk. Rollers of dust moved across the bare wooden floor, stirred by the breeze from the open window.

"Well, where should we look?" asked Fergie hoarsely. He was still whispering, and with good reason: The study was at the front of the house, and through the open window they could hear the policemen and the others talking down on the front walk.

"How should I know?" Johnny shot back. "Why don't you check out that table by the door? There're some papers on it, and they might be important. I'll have a look at the desk."

Cautiously, with many nervous glances toward the window, Johnny edged around behind the desk. He scanned the things on the desktop, and he noticed, with amusement, that the professor had written a crabby comment on the exam book that lay at the top of the heap. He had given the exam a grade of C minus, and he had scrawled a few words in red ink on the blue cover: *If you could possibly learn to write decent English, you might be able to unscramble your mixed-up . . .* But this was as far as the professor had gotten. His last word had ended with a sharp downstroke of the pen, and at the end of the stroke was a hole, as if the professor had jammed the pen down hard into the book. Near the book lay the professor's green Estabrook fountain pen. The pen point was badly bent.

Johnny pondered this clue, wondering what it might mean. While he was thinking, his gaze wandered. Was there anything more that would help them in any way?

Part of the desktop was covered by a green blotter, on which the professor had doodled his usual geometric patterns and flowers and funny faces. To the left of the blotter stood a small bronze bowl with rubber bands and paper clips and a large green rubber eraser in it. And there was a glass paperweight full of sand from the Great Desert of Maine, a rack of pipes, a gray Balkan Sobranie tobacco can, and a large, tasteless cigarette lighter shaped like a knight in armor. Johnny felt confused and disheartened. There weren't any big fat clues staring him in the face, were there? But then detective work was not supposed to be easy. He pursed his lips and glanced to his left. He noticed something that he hadn't noticed before.

Over in the corner, behind the floor lamp, was a dictionary stand. It looked like a lectern, with a screw mechanism that allowed you to raise or lower it. Propped up on the slanted top was a lined yellow notepad, and the top sheet was entirely covered by a large drawing. It looked like this:

Johnny stared at the drawing. It was done in pencil, and the drawing style was definitely the professor's. But what made the whole thing so odd was this: The professor never did huge drawings. His doodles were always small, like the ones on the desk blotter. So why had he done this sketch, which looked like a capital letter *L* wreathed about with a vine? Was he trying to say something? And if so, what?

Fergie's voice cut in on Johnny's thoughts. "Hey, Dixon!" he hissed. "We better get outa here! I mean, those cops might decide to come back in and have another look around. Didja find anything?"

Johnny sighed. "Nope. Not much. I'm gonna take this drawing back with us. It might be a clue. You're right, though—we better make ourselves scarce. C'mon!"

CHAPTER FOUR

That afternoon Fergie and Johnny got together down at the public library. They were supposed to be doing their homework, but they were actually there to compare notes about their visit to the professor's study. Naturally they couldn't sit in the main reading room and babble at each other. So they went to the upper level of the stacks, where they could stand behind the rows of iron bookshelves and talk in a fairly normal tone of voice. Unfortunately, they soon found that they really did not have a lot to discuss. Fergie had found absolutely nothing, and Johnny had only come up with two things that he thought were of any importance: the pen and the drawing. Fergie was not impressed by either of these "clues."

"So what if he did mash up the point of his pen?" he asked in a bored tone. "Everybody knows he's got a rotten temper. You told me he throws dishes sometimes when he gets mad."

"Yeah, but the dishes are from the ten-cent store," Johnny replied. "He never breaks anything that he really likes. And he was crazy about that pen. He used to keep it in a special case in his desk. It's wrecked now—didja see the way the point looked?" Johnny crossed the index finger and the middle finger of his right hand to show how the two parts of the gold-plated nib had gotten crossed. "He would *never* have done that on purpose!" Johnny added insistently.

"So how do you think the pen got busted?" Fergie asked.

Johnny shrugged. "I dunno."

There was an awkward pause, and then Johnny spoke up again.

"I think that drawing I showed you might be the only real clue we have. But I can't figure out what it means."

Fergie shrugged. "Oh, what the heck, let's see it, Dixon. Didja bring it with you?"

"Uh huh." Johnny took his Latin book out from under his arm. He opened it and pulled out a folded square of lined yellow paper. Unfolding it carefully, he handed the drawing to Fergie.

Fergie examined the picture, humming all the while. Suddenly he snapped his fingers. "Hey! I bet I know what this is! It's a *rebus*! You know what a rebus is?"

Johnny felt insulted. He was proud of all the obscure facts that he knew, and he knew about rebuses. A rebus was when you used objects and letters to represent somebody's name. Rebuses appeared in coats of arms, like the two gates (two-door) that were used as a symbol for the royal house of Tudor.

"Yeah, I know about rebuses, an' I probably know more about 'em than you do!" said Johnny irritably. "So what does this represent? Huh?"

Fergie smiled smugly. "Well, there's an *L* and there's a vine. Put 'em together and you get L-vine. *Levine!* Smart, eh?"

Johnny thought about this for a bit. "Ye-ah, it *might* be . . ." he said slowly. "But where does that get us? I don't think I ever heard the professor mention anybody named Levine. I would've remembered it if he had."

Fergie looked disappointed. But he persisted. "Okay, so you never heard of anybody he knew that was named Levine. So what does that prove? Maybe some guy outa his deep dark past, some gangster named Itchy Thumb Levine, came an' kidnapped him, because the prof owed him some dough. Makes sense, doesn't it?"

Johnny turned to Fergie wearily. The look on his face showed total despair. "You still don't believe I saw his face in that mirror, do you?" he asked. "You just can't admit that it could've been a ghost or a wizard that took the professor away. You've gotta have some kind of one hundred percent proof, or you won't believe *anything*!"

Fergie stared at the floor. "I think we oughta go down

an' finish our homework," he muttered. "We're not gettin' anywhere on this thing!"

"No, I guess we're not," said Johnny gloomily. He was up against a stone wall, and he knew it. He felt angry at Fergie for being so skeptical. Johnny was utterly convinced that he had seen the professor's anguished face in that bedroom mirror. It hadn't been a panicky hallucination or the result of bad nerves or anything like that. But even if Fergie had accepted Johnny's version of the story, where would that leave them? Nowhere. Absolutely nowhere.

Days passed. Weeks passed. The professor became a Missing Person. His picture was shown on TV and printed in the newspapers. His description was read aloud on the radio several times a day. Ponds and rivers were dragged, and forests were searched. But no leads turned up. He hadn't taken his car—it was still parked in his garage. Most of his clothes were still hanging in his bedroom closet. His suitcases gathered dust in his attic. Wherever he had gone to, he had taken the clothes on his back and not much more.

As time went by Johnny began to miss the professor a lot. It was as if a big piece of his life had been swept away. He missed the professor's cranky comments on everything under the sun. He missed the chocolate cakes and the chess games and the long discussions about history and war and politics and life in general. He missed this strange, eccentric, good-hearted old man who had been such a wonderful friend to him. Every day as he walked home from school Johnny would stop and stare at the professor's house. It looked shut up, abandoned. The blinds were drawn, and already some kid in the neighborhood had taken good aim with a rock and had broken an attic window. Sometimes Johnny would stare up at the ridiculous, ramshackle radio aerial on the roof of the cupola. The professor had built it so he could pick up the Red Sox broadcasts better. Whenever he saw the aerial, tears sprang to Johnny's eyes. And then he felt angry and frustrated and wished he were able to wave a magic wand and summon the professor back from wherever he was. But he couldn't do that, and more and more, as the days passed, he began to feel that the old man was probably gone for good.

One Tuesday early in May Johnny was called out of school to help serve at a funeral. Johnny went to a Catholic school, and for him, going to church was very much a part of school life. The church stood right next to the school, and Johnny had been trained as an altar boy. Altar boys help the priest when he says Mass: they light candles and bring him books and cruets of water and wine. To serve at an ordinary daily Mass only two boys are needed. But at a funeral Mass you need at least five: two to carry candles, one to carry the tall gilded cross that is mounted on a pole, and two to carry the censer and the incense bowl as the priest walks around the coffin and offers incense smoke to it. After the service one of the boys rides out to the cemetery with the priest and hands him the holy water sprinkler and the prayer book when the priest says the final prayers at the edge of the grave.

On this particular day Johnny rode out to the cemetery in a big black Cadillac that belonged to the Digby and Coughlan Funeral Home. The driver was a solemn-looking young man in a black suit. Johnny sat in back with Father Higgins, the pastor of St. Michael's church, who was a tall, glowering man with grizzled gray hair and a squarish jaw. He was an old friend of the professor's—Johnny had seen them playing pinochle and arguing many, many times. During the Second World War, Father Higgins had been an army chaplain, and he had been wounded in a battle on the small Pacific island of Guam, which he always pronounced *Goo*-ahm. The war had given Father Higgins a permanent case of bad nerves and a violent temper, and half the kids at St. Michael's school were scared to death of him. Johnny had always gotten along with him, however; partly it was because he was mild-mannered and never gave Father Higgins a hard time. And partly it was because Johnny really knew his Latin and could rattle it off at a furious pace during the church services, without stopping or stumbling over words. As he sat next to the priest in the car an odd notion came floating into Johnny's mind: Maybe he could get Father Higgins to help him find the professor.

At first this thought seemed so ridiculous to Johnny

that he almost laughed out loud. But the more he thought, the more logical the idea seemed: after all, priests were involved in magic. The rituals they performed in church were sort of like magic rituals, and they recited long incantations in Latin that were almost like spells. And Johnny knew that Father Higgins believed in ghosts, witches, vampires, and things of that sort—he was always telling stories about weird and uncanny things that had happened to friends or relatives of his. Unlike Fergie, he would not insist on having everything proved beyond a shadow of a doubt. Anyway, it was worth a try—*anything* was worth a try at this stage of the game. So later, as they were driving back to the church, he decided to take the plunge.

"Uh . . . Father?" he said hesitantly.

Father Higgins was reading his breviary, which is a small black book full of prayers. He looked up, startled. "Hm? Oh! Yes, John? What is it?"

Johnny screwed his face up into several funny expressions. He was just too afraid to tackle this question head-on. Instead he approached it in a roundabout way.

"Father? Er . . . what would you do if you had lost something really valuable and you wanted to get it back?"

Father Higgins closed his book and smiled thoughtfully. "Well," he said, "I know it's just a superstition, but I would pray to Saint Anthony. I lost my keys in the rectory one day, and I prayed to Saint Anthony, and I found 'em right away. You're not *really* supposed to believe in stuff like that, but all the same . . . well, I'd give it a try if I were you. I really would."

Johnny was startled. He really hadn't expected a suggestion of this kind. Of course, he knew about Saint Anthony: He was the patron saint of lost objects. Johnny's grandma was always praying to the saint to help her find pins, needles, and lost money. But could Saint Anthony help you find a lost *person*?

There was silence in the car for a while. Father Higgins laid the book down on the seat and dug his hand into the pocket of his black overcoat. He pulled out a stubby briar pipe with a silver band on the stem. With an odd smile on his face, he turned the pipe over in his hands. Then he glanced suddenly at Johnny—it was a keen, piercing, unnerving glance.

"Of course," he said in an insinuating tone, "if you're looking for lost *people*—lost professors, for instance—there is a ritual that folks use. It's full of hocus-pocus and it's totally unreliable, but it might just be worth a try."

Johnny looked at the priest and blushed. Father Higgins had read his thoughts. The priest was laughing, and Johnny did too. It was a relief to laugh—he had been pretty tense about this whole business.

"I ought to've known that I couldn't put one over on you, Father," said Johnny shyly.

"Darned right you can't," said the priest, still chuckling. "And anyway, the professor is my friend too. I miss him a lot." He paused and added sadly, "I think he was probably one of the few real friends I had in the whole wide world."

Johnny was only half-listening to what Father Higgins was saying. He was all worked up about the "ritual" that Father Higgins had mentioned, and he wanted to quiz him about it. "Father?" he said hesitantly. "What about . . . I mean, you mentioned a ritual of some kind. I wondered if maybe—"

"Ah, yes!" said the priest, cheering up suddenly. He began to study the bowl of his pipe as if there were dark secrets hidden there. "I did mention something of that sort, didn't I? Well, I know I'm going to sound like a superstitious old Irishman, but I think I would leave a petition under the base of the statue of Saint Anthony in our church. You know the statue I mean, don't you?"

Johnny nodded. He knew it well. It was a large painted plaster figure that stood on a pedestal in front of one of the pillars in St. Michael's church.

"Well, then," the priest went on in a conspiratorial tone, "how about if you and I meet in the church this coming Wednesday night, after the service? This was something that I was going to try myself, but I kept thinking that it was an idiotic notion. However, now that you've put the flea in my ear, I'm a bit more eager to try. I have a few little extra—hrrumph!—things to throw in, just to make the ritual more, uh, *effective*. Not that I think we'll get any results worth writing home about, but—as they say—it can't hurt."

Johnny believed in superstitious practices and magic

more than the average kid did. And it seemed logical to him to think that maybe the professor could be located and saved by a magical rite. After all, his disappearance had been surrounded by strange supernatural omens and signs. If magic had snatched him away, maybe magic could bring him back.

And so, when Wednesday evening came around, Johnny went off to St. Michael's church. Every Wednesday night during the month of May special services were held in the church in honor of Mary, the mother of Christ. Normally Johnny did not go to these services, so Gramma and Grampa Dixon were quite surprised when he told them he was attending. Gramma would have gone with him, but she had a cold, and she was afraid the night air would make it worse. Johnny was immensely relieved that she wasn't going: he felt nervous and embarrassed about what he was doing, and he wanted as few spectators as possible when he and Father Higgins did their mumbo jumbo. All through the service his mind was elsewhere. He kept thinking, *Will it work?* Well, he'd know fairly soon.

The service ended, and the people filed out of the church. When Johnny was sure that he was alone, he got up and walked to the front of the church and stood before the statue of Saint Anthony. It was about six feet high, and since it stood on a tall pedestal, it towered over him. The statue showed Saint Anthony as a monk in a brown robe. He was holding a book in one hand; the other hand was raised in a blessing. There was a gilt halo behind his head, and on his face was a blank, wide-eyed stare. Before the statue stood an iron rack with flickering candles in it. People had lit them in honor of the saint, so that he would answer their petitions.

Johnny fidgeted and glanced around. He felt silly, but he reminded himself that Father Higgins was in on this too. But where was he? Probably he was in the sacristy, which was the room where the priest got dressed for Mass and other services. Maybe he had decided that the whole thing was a bad idea and had therefore gone home. Johnny hoped that this was not the case. He fidgeted some more. He drummed his fingers on his legs and walked back and forth, humming softly under his breath. At last he heard the sound of the sacristy door opening and closing. He looked up and saw Father Higgins walking toward him. He was wearing a long white gown called an alb, and around his neck was a kind of embroidered purple scarf called a stole. In one hand he carried a tarnished silver holy water sprinkler. In the other he carried a small pad of paper and a pencil. Johnny was surprised to see that the priest was just as nervous as he was—he kept glancing toward the back of the church to see if anyone was watching.

"Here," said Father Higgins gruffly, and he shoved the pad and pencil at Johnny. He turned toward Saint Anthony and bowed and then walked closer to the statue, raised his hands in a gesture of supplication, and rattled off a prayer in Latin. Johnny did not understand much of it, but he heard the words *Sanctus Antonius* several times, and he figured that the priest was calling on Saint Anthony to hear their prayers. Raising the sprinkler, Father Higgins shook drops of holy water over the base of the statue. Some water fell on the burning candles, which hissed loudly. Again the priest bowed, and once more he turned to Johnny.

"All right, here's what you do," he said brusquely, tapping the pad with his finger. "Write down your petition, fold the paper over twice, and hand it to me."

Johnny raised the pencil and wrote:

> *Dear Saint Anthony:*
> *Please help us to find Professor*
> *Childermass. Please hear us, and do*
> *not fail us. Amen.*
>
> > *Yours truly,*
> > *John Dixon*

Johnny tore the sheet from the pad and folded it twice. He handed the note to Father Higgins, who asked him to hold the holy water sprinkler for a minute. While Johnny watched, the priest edged in between the candle rack and the statue's pedestal. Reaching up, he placed a brawny hand on the front of the statue and tilted it slightly back. With his other hand he stuffed the note in under the base of the statue. Then, gently, he lowered the statue back down. Johnny heard a soft *chink* as the statue came to rest on its pedestal again. Grunting a little, Father Higgins squeezed himself out from behind the candle rack and walked back to where Johnny was standing. He took the sprinkler from Johnny, showered the statue with more water, and then said another Latin prayer.

"*There!*" he said wearily, folding his arms and stepping back to watch the play of candle shadows on the statue's pallid face. "I didn't think I could remember all that razzmatazz, but I did! And if you *ever* tell anyone in the parish that we did this, I'll have your hide! I think Bishop Monohan would go through the roof if he knew I was such a slave to mummery and flummery!"

Johnny was genuinely grateful for what Father Higgins had done tonight. Whether or not the ritual worked, at least they had tried. However, there were still some lingering questions in his mind.

"What do we do now, Father?" he asked. "I mean, how do we know if what we did worked or not?"

Father Higgins sighed. "I might have known you'd ask that! Well, we're supposed to wait three days and then come back and see what—if anything—is written on the paper. If the saint answers us, he will answer us in that way."

Johnny looked at the priest doubtfully. "Has . . . has this ever worked before? Did anyone ever—"

"No," said the priest with a mournful shake of his head. "Not that I ever heard of, anyway. But as I told you the other day, there's no harm in—"

Suddenly there was a loud sound, like a pistol shot. A door at the back of the church blew open, and it banged loudly against the wall. A cold wind blew in, and the candle flames flickered. Johnny jumped. With a wild look on his face, he peered into the darkness, and then he turned and gaped at Father Higgins. The expression on the priest's face was absolutely unreadable, but his eyes were gleaming. And Johnny wondered: *Was this a sign? Would their prayer really be answered?*

CHAPTER FIVE

For the time being Johnny was not getting any answers. "Stupid door blew open again," muttered Father Higgins, and he stamped on down the aisle to close it.

Three days they had to wait. For Johnny, three days had seldom passed so slowly. Thursday dragged by, and so did Friday. On Friday evening, to make himself feel better, Johnny called up Father Higgins and had a long conversation with him. He had not wanted to talk about the ghostly jack-o'-lantern before for fear that the priest might laugh at him. But now he decided to lay the whole thing out on the table. He told Father Higgins what he had seen, and he described the night when he burst into the professor's house and found that he had vanished. And he added that he was afraid that evil supernatural powers had had something to do with the professor's disappearance. He also mentioned the Childermass clock and told Father Higgins a little about its strange history. But he did not mention the ghostly midnight vision he had had or the skull—these were things that he still wanted to keep secret. Father Higgins listened gravely to what Johnny had to say, and he did not scoff or laugh. He said that Johnny was probably right, that deviltry was almost certainly involved, and he added encouragingly that the powers of light might come to their aid. They'd know on Saturday night.

Finally Saturday evening arrived. There was no church service scheduled for that night, so Johnny said that he was going to light a candle in memory of his mother. When he got to St. Michael's church, he immediately scooted around the block to the rectory, which was where Father Higgins lived. He pushed the door bell, and soon the priest came, holding in his hand a bunch of keys to all the various doors and locked cupboards of St. Michael's church. Father Higgins looked tense and crabby.

"Well," he said, scowling, "I suppose we might as well go see what we can see. I warn you, though: There may be nothing written on the sheet at all—nothing, that is, but the message you wrote the other night."

Johnny had already prepared himself for disappointment. This was a silly, crazy thing they were doing, and he knew it. He told himself not to expect too much.

Father Higgins and Johnny entered the church by a

side door. The old building smelled of wax and incense, and the air was clammy, as it always was, even in the middle of the summer. All around them the dark, empty church loomed. Half a dozen candles burned in the slanted, wax-encrusted iron rack in front of Saint Anthony. As Father Higgins walked toward the statue, Johnny could feel himself growing tense. The priest slid between the candle rack and the pedestal and placed one large, hairy hand on the front of the statue. Johnny heard him mutter something as he tilted the heavy statue back. His fingers were on the folded paper now, and he was yanking it out. Down came the statue again, gently clunking into place. Father Higgins squeezed himself out from behind the rack; he walked toward Johnny with the paper in his hand. The suspense was unbearable. Johnny clenched his fists and felt his nails digging into the palms of his hands. With maddening slowness Father Higgins unfolded the paper. He looked at it, and then he let out a loud exclamation.

"Good God! Come and look at this, would you!"

Johnny edged closer and peered over the priest's arm. Across the note that he had neatly printed was writing. It was large, scrawly, and loopy script, and it reminded Johnny of the marks he had made once when he'd tried to write while holding a pencil in his teeth. At first the writing looked like total nonsense, but Johnny soon realized that there were words and phrases. With a little effort he was able to make out what they said:

Father Higgins's jaw sagged. "Lord!" he whispered. "I would never in my wildest dreams have believed—" Suddenly he stopped speaking. His eyes narrowed, and he turned around and peered into the gloom.

"What's the matter, Father?" asked Johnny, frightened.

"Oh, it was just a thought that occurred to me," muttered the priest. "I wondered if maybe somebody had been hiding in the church and watching when we put this note under the statue. If they had been, they might've taken the note out and written this."

Johnny's heart sank. He knew that this might be the real, true explanation behind the mysterious writing. But he did not want to believe it. "Gee, Father," he said hopefully, "I think the church was empty that night, wasn't it? I mean, didn't we check it out?"

The priest shook his head. "No, John. That's just the trouble—we did *not* check it out. There could've been somebody up in the choir loft or squatting down behind the pews. You know Raymond—that feeble-minded guy that works at the gas station across the street? Well, he could've been in here. He ducks into the church sometimes and does funny things, like movin' the candles around on the altar. And now that I think about it, that might explain the front door bangin' open the other night. I wonder . . ."

Johnny was beginning to feel desperate. If Father Higgins didn't believe this was real supernatural writing, then who would help him find the professor? "I . . . I don't think R-Raymond could've . . . m-moved the statue. . . ." said Johnny in a voice that was beginning to tremble. Tears sprang to his eyes, and he could feel his lower lip quivering. He didn't want to break down and cry, but he was afraid he was going to.

Father Higgins turned to Johnny, and his harsh scowl softened into a sympathetic, sad smile. He really was a kind-hearted man, and he realized how much Johnny wanted to believe that the writing had been done by supernatural powers.

"Look, John," said the priest softly, putting his arm around him. "I'm not tryin' to be mean to you. I'm just tryin' to test out this thing and see if maybe there's an ordinary, everyday explanation to it. I believe in miracles, but they sure don't happen all the time. We've got to keep our heads if we're going to get anywhere."

Johnny was crying now—he couldn't help it. The tears flowed freely, and he dabbed at his eyes with his handkerchief. "Does . . . does that mean you're not gonna help me anymore?" he sobbed.

"Of *course* not!" said the priest loudly and firmly. "Whatever gave you *that* idea? I want to find the professor just as much as you do!" He paused and rubbed his chin, and then he looked at the scrawling on the paper again. Suddenly he grinned. He laughed aloud, and the sound echoed in the vaulted ceiling of the old church.

Johnny took his handkerchief away from his face and blinked. "What . . . what is it?" he asked in a voice that was thick from crying.

"Oh, nothing much," said the priest, still chuckling. "Only I realized all of a sudden that I'd have to be out of my mind to think that Raymond did this! That second sentence there, about the great reckoning in the little room. It's from a play by Shakespeare. Old Raymond might be able to read and write, but he sure didn't write *this*! I ought to've seen that right away!"

Johnny's heart leaped. He was feeling hopeful again. "Does that mean the writing is really from . . . from . . ."

Father Higgins cut him off with a shake of his head. "No. It doesn't mean anything. Somebody else could've done this for all we know. But I don't think we ought to throw this paper away. No, indeed! We ought to study it and think about it and take it very, very seriously. Because you never know! It just might be a miracle from Saint Anthony! And if it is, it could help us find the professor. Anyway, we've got to take the help that's given to us. Like they say, beggars can't be choosers!"

Johnny went home that night thinking that maybe—just maybe—there was some reason to hope. It was possible that Saint Anthony or some higher power had spoken. But whoever it was, he or she had not spoken very clearly. *Where the bays run together*—what could that mean? It seemed to refer to a place, but where? There were lots of bays on the surface of the globe. Johnny knew the names of some of them: Hudson Bay, the Bay of Fundy, Corpus Christi Bay. Was there some place where two bays of water ran into one? He could start combing through an atlas, but it would be like looking for a needle in a haystack. Then Johnny thought some more: He had heard horses referred to as *bays*. They were horses that were reddish-brown in color. Did the clue mean that they should look for some field full of reddish-brown horses? Then there was the other clue: *a great reckoning in a little room.* The "little room" had to be the dollhouse room in the Childermass clock. But except for this little glimmer of meaning, the phrase meant absolutely nothing to Johnny. He turned it over and over in his mind, but the more he thought, the more meaningless the phrase became.

By the time he got to his front door, Johnny's hopeful mood had evaporated. He remembered the things he had read about the Greek oracles, which had given people mysterious messages just to drive them bats. Maybe the messages had been sent by the devil and not by Saint Anthony. Maybe they were stuck up against a dead-end wall.

The next day was Sunday, and Johnny went to church with his gramma and grampa as usual. After Mass everybody filed out of the church. Some went home right away, but others stood around outside and talked with their friends. Gramma and Grampa got into a conversation with Mrs. McGinnis, a silly old lady who was the head of the Catholic Daughters. Johnny couldn't stand Mrs. McGinnis, and so he just stood by, fidgeting nervously and waiting for his grandparents to finish talking. But as he was glancing aimlessly this way and that, Johnny saw Willie Prine elbowing his way through the crowd. Willie was a tall, dopey-looking kid with thick glasses, and he had been one of the altar boys at today's Mass. He was still wearing his long red cassock, and he was grinning from ear to ear. Johnny wondered what he was so pleased about.

"Hey, Dixon!" yelled Willie. "Father Higgins wants ta see ya!" Willie chortled. He was bubbling over with malicious amusement. Obviously Willie thought that Johnny was in trouble, and that pleased him no end. He didn't have anything in particular against Johnny—he just liked seeing other kids get bawled out.

When they heard what Willie was saying, Gramma and Grampa both looked upset. Mrs. McGinnis clucked and acted prissy, as she always did when bad things happened to other people. Johnny, however, was calm. He turned and smiled smugly at Willie.

"Okay," he said quietly. "I'll be with you in a minute." Then he turned back to Gramma and Grampa. "I have to go see Father Higgins about something," he said quickly. "It's . . . it's not very important, it's just about the altar boy schedule. You go ahead—I'll walk home afterward."

Before his grandparents had a chance to say anything, Johnny was plunging off into the crowd behind Willie. The expression on Willie's face showed that he was perplexed. Why was Dixon so eager to go and get chewed out? When they got to the door of the sacristy, there was Father Higgins. The iron doors of the big Mosler walk-in safe were open, and he was putting away the sacred vessels—the chalice, the ciborium, and the gold-plated paten. As the two boys watched, he swung the squealing doors shut and locked them.

"Good morning, John!" said the priest, turning to face him. His eyes were gleaming, and there was a secretive smile on his face. "How goes it with you today, eh?"

"Uh . . . okay, I guess, Father." Johnny's mouth twitched into a nervous smile. Even though the priest was his friend, he often felt nervous around him. Anybody who was in authority gave Johnny the jitters. "Did . . . did you want to talk to me about something?"

"I did indeed!" the priest replied, and his voice sounded ominous. At this Willie smirked expectantly. Now Dixon was going to get it! But to his great surprise, Willie suddenly found the priest glaring at him.

"Well, Mr. Prine," he growled, "I don't think I need you any longer. You had better put out the candles, change into your clothes, and go home."

Willie's face fell. "Uh . . . yeah, sure, Father. See ya later." And with that, he turned and went out, closing the door behind him.

Now Johnny and Father Higgins were alone in the sacristy. At first the priest said nothing. He walked over to the tall walnut dresser where the Mass vestments were kept. On top of the dresser was a heavy iron crucifix. Next to it lay a neatly folded road map. As Johnny watched, Father Higgins picked up the map. He held it up so that Johnny could see the title on the front. It was a road map of the state of Maine.

"I've been doing some thinking about those two little messages that Saint Anthony scrawled down for us," he said, tapping the map against the edge of the dresser. "And you know, all of a sudden, last night at dinner, it came to me! I should've thought of it before, because I have hundreds and hundreds of folk songs rattling around in my head. Here, hold this!"

To Johnny's surprise, Father Higgins handed him the map. Then he turned and strode quickly to the coat closet in the far corner of the room. Opening the door, he reached in and pulled out—a guitar!

Johnny's mouth dropped open. He was completely dumbfounded and also very amused. So Father Higgins played the guitar! He normally looked so stern and forbidding that . . . well, it was like finding out that the mayor loved to roller-skate! As Johnny watched, the priest put the strap of the guitar around his neck, played a few opening chords, and then launched into a loud, lusty chorus:

Haul down your sails where the bays run together,
While away your days in the hills of Isle au Haut!

Father Higgins clamped his hand over the strings, and they were silent. "There!" he said triumphantly. "That's it! You get it, don't you?"

Johnny was still mystified. It was clear that one of the lines they had found was from a song. But Johnny did not have the faintest idea of where the hills of Isle au Haut were.

Father Higgins looked at Johnny askance. His lips curled up into a sarcastic grin. "Oh, come on, now! You don't know where Isle au Haut is? You really don't know?"

Johnny shrugged helplessly. "I'm from Long Island, Father! I . . . I don't know very much about New England. Is Isle au Haut someplace in Maine? I mean, there are islands along the coast of Maine, aren't there?"

Father Higgins laughed. "Is it someplace in Maine? Are there islands along the coast? Is the Pope a Catholic? Holy Saint Patrick! You outlanders don't know *anything* about New England, do you?"

Johnny felt sheepish. "Nope, I guess not," he muttered.

"Well, here! I'll show you!" said the priest, and he took off the guitar and leaned it against the dresser. Taking the map from Johnny's hands, he unfolded it and held it up. Father Higgins's large hairy forefinger moved along the coast of Maine, which even on a map looked as if it had had big chunks chewed or ripped out of it. Far up the coast, Johnny saw the two long bays that had been scooped out of the shoreline millions of years ago: Penobscot Bay and Blue Hill Bay. Both bays were full of islands large and small. But at the place where the two bays met was a cluster of islands and islets. Even though the priest was holding the map at a slight distance, Johnny's nearsighted eyes could pick out the names of the larger ones. On the left were two together —the one above was North Haven, and below it was Vinalhaven. Then, slightly to the east of these two, was another fair-sized island called Isle au Haut.

Johnny looked up wonderingly at Father Higgins. "You mean . . . you think the professor is out here somewhere?"

Father Higgins nodded. "That is indeed what I think. But whereabouts in this ungodly wilderness of islands he is, God only knows."

Johnny gazed at the map, and then he shook his head sadly. "But why, Father? I mean, I don't understand why anybody would kidnap the professor and take him out to one of these islands."

Father Higgins looked grave. He folded the map back up and laid it on the dresser. "Neither do I, Johnny. Neither do I. It may not even be a some*body* that's done it—from all that you've told me, it is more likely to be a some*thing* that did it. One of the powers of darkness, in other words. We'll know more when we get to the islands, I suppose, and by that time we may wish that we knew less. Of course, there's always the possibility that he's *not* out on these blasted islands, but the more I think, the more sure I am that we're on the right track. You see, I've doped out the other clue too. And it leads us right to Vinalhaven Island!"

Johnny's mouth dropped open. "Huh?"

Father Higgins scratched his nose and grinned. "Well

you may say, 'huh'! I'll admit it isn't terribly apparent at first, but I'll tell you what I did. You see, I figured that *a great reckoning in a little room* had to refer to that blasted dollhouse you told me about. And I'm sure you reached the same conclusion. Anyway, I called up the owner of the Fitzwilliam Inn to see if we could . . . you know, kind of make an appointment to examine that clock and see what we could find out. And do you know what he told me? He told me that he had sold the clock to a guy who runs a clock museum. The guy's name is Herman Finnick, and his museum is out on Vinalhaven Island! Now, doesn't that just beat everything?"

Johnny nodded. He felt stunned by all the information that had suddenly been dumped on him. And then it was as if a light had come on inside his brain. He snapped his fingers. "Hey, Father!" he exclaimed. "It all fits!"

Father Higgins blinked. "Huh? What fits?"

Johnny grinned. "When a friend of mine and I were pokin' around in the professor's study after he disappeared, we found this drawing that showed a letter *L* with a vine wrapped around it. My friend thought that it stood for *L* plus vine—the name Levine, I mean. But we should've read it the other way around: it's Vine-L, for Vinalhaven!"

"Very good!" said Father Higgins, nodding approvingly. "And that also settles a question that has been banging around in my skull: I was wondering whether we ought to go to Isle au Haut, since it gets mentioned in that little ditty I sang for you. But all the signs seem to point to Vinalhaven, don't they?" Father Higgins paused. "Hmmm!" he said, grimly pounding his fist on the edge of the dresser. "What does that Finnick character have to do with it all? He *must* be in on this plot to do something to the professor. Is this Finnick a sorcerer? Is he in league with the devil? Did he create the jack-o'-lantern vision that you saw? And why on earth does he want the professor? What awful, ghastly, unnameable thing is going to happen to the poor man? As far as I'm concerned, there are about six hundred and fifty unanswered questions in this whole nutty business!" The priest turned suddenly to Johnny and pointed a knobby, hairy finger at him. His face had turned beet-red, and he looked very threatening and sinister. Johnny cringed. He was afraid that Father Higgins was going to yell at him or grab him by the shoulders and shake him.

"What I want to know now, John, is *this*!" roared the priest. "Are you going with me to Vinalhaven to help rescue the prof? What d'ye say?"

CHAPTER SIX

Johnny was overjoyed. He wanted to yell and whoop and throw things around the room. Father Higgins had told him the thing that he wanted most in the world to hear. He was saying that they had a chance to find the professor and rescue him, and what was more, he was saying that he wanted him, John Dixon, to be his right-hand man in this search. If he hadn't been such a polite and well-behaved kid, Johnny would have thrown his arms around the tall, grizzly faced priest. As it was, he just stood there looking grateful, tears streaming down his face.

"Th-thanks, F-Father," he stammered in a voice thick with emotion. "I . . . I'll help you if I can."

Father Higgins smiled happily. He was a pretty

shrewd judge of character, and he had guessed that—underneath his timid exterior—Johnny was a courageous and resourceful kid. However, he didn't want Johnny to think that this expedition of theirs was going to be all fun and games. So he forced himself to frown and be gruff again.

"You may not thank me when this little jaunt is over with," he rumbled. "We may find that we're up against something that we can't handle, or we may not even be able to locate the professor at all. But if people tried to do only those things that they were sure of succeeding at, this country would still be a howling wilderness. Anyway, I'm going to need help—lots of help—and I'm very glad you want to go along. Unfortunately, next weekend is the soonest I can get away. I'll have to phone the bishop's office and ask them to send out a substitute. Do you think your gramma and grampa will let you go on this trip with me?"

"I . . . I guess they'll let me go," he said uncertainly.

"I'll call up your folks and tell them that I'm taking you on a little pleasure jaunt," the priest said, and smiled wryly. "And I'm sure," he added, "that God will forgive me for fibbing a bit, if it's all in a good cause. Now, if you'll excuse me, I have to be getting on over to the Tip Top restaurant for lunch. Father Frisbie of St. Luke's Episcopal is meeting me, and we're going to stuff ourselves with corned beef and cabbage and argue about religion."

Johnny went home in a daze. It took him a day or two

to get used to the idea that he was going on a rescue mission with the rector of St. Michael's church. At times the whole thing seemed unreal to him, and when he thought that they were going because of mysterious words scribbled on a piece of paper that had been left under a statue in a church . . . well, he didn't know whether to laugh or cry. But the trip was actually going to happen. Father Higgins called up the Dixons and discussed the matter with them, and they seemed perfectly willing to let Johnny go. As far as they were concerned, Father Higgins was a reliable, upstanding member of the community, and they were both quite proud that he had chosen Johnny to go with him on a short trip to the islands off the coast of Maine. Gramma and Grampa knew that Johnny was feeling bad because of the professor's disappearance, and they hoped this jaunt would help him get his mind off that sad loss.

So Johnny got out his small, squarish plaid suitcase and started putting things in it: pajamas, toiletries, extra socks, and his best warm woolen sweaters and flannel shirts—it was still pretty chilly in May on those islands, as Gramma kept pointing out. Johnny threw in other odd but useful things, like his waterproof matchbox, his three-bladed jackknife, his Boy Scout compass, and an old battered pair of opera glasses that could be used as a set of binoculars. After some hesitation he decided to put in the "lucky" skull from the Childermass clock.

Johnny didn't quite know what to think about the skull. He had begun to have bad feelings about it lately, for no reason that he could really put his finger on. And he found that he was still being extremely close-mouthed about the skull. He hadn't told Fergie or Father Higgins or any of his friends about it. His mind kept making up reasons why it would be better to keep the skull a secret, at least for a little while longer. If he told Fergie, he might want to steal it. As for Father Higgins, well, Johnny told himself that it would not be a great idea to let your parish priest know that you had swiped something. But then what *should* he do about the skull? Leave it to gather dust forever in his bureau drawer? Arguing back and forth with himself, Johnny finally came back to the notion that the skull might just possibly be lucky. And so he dug the watchcase that held the grotesque object out from under the shirts in his bureau drawer and stuffed it in under the other things in his suitcase. *There!* he said quietly to himself. *I hope you're a good-luck charm, skully baby. Because if I ever needed some good luck, I'm gonna need it now!*

On the Tuesday after his conversation with Father Higgins, Johnny made a big mistake—at least, it seemed like a mistake to him at the time. He spilled the beans to Fergie about the trip that he and the priest were going to take. At first Johnny had kept his mouth shut about the whole enterprise. He hadn't even told Fergie about the mysterious messages that he and Father Higgins had found under Saint Anthony's statue. He hadn't told him because he had been kind of ticked off at him. Fergie had been smart-alecky and sneery about the weird magical happenings that had surrounded the professor's disappearance, and he had demanded proof positive before believing. So Johnny had simply cut him out of the professor-finding project. He had not asked Fergie's advice on this matter lately, and he really had not seen much of him since the night they discussed clues together in the public library. They had met at Peter's Sweet Shop a couple of times since then, but mostly they had just talked about girls, the Red Sox, and homework. Johnny did not feel good about shutting Fergie out. Smart aleck or not, Fergie was his friend. As the Vinalhaven trip got closer, Johnny felt an overpowering urge to let him in on what was going on, regardless of what the result might be.

And so, on Tuesday evening after school, Johnny decided to tell all. They were facing each other across ice cream sundaes at Peter's, and Fergie was going on about how Wanda Sue Geiger was the prettiest girl in the eighth grade. Suddenly Johnny cut in.

"Hey, look, Fergie!" he said, jamming his spoon into the ice cream. "I . . . I've got something to tell you."

Fergie stopped talking and stared levelly across at Johnny. "Yeah," he said. "I know you have!"

Johnny was startled. "You *do*?"

"Yes, I do! Good God, Dixon! You must think I have whipped cream where my brain is supposed to be! You've been givin' me these funny looks, an' peerin' at me squinty-eyed for a coupla weeks now! I thought maybe you were gettin' ready to enlist in the French

Foreign Legion or somethin'! An' I don't mind tellin' you, I got pretty mad at you. After all, I'm supposed to be your best friend, aren't I? Well, aren't I?"

Johnny blushed a deep crimson. He felt stupid and guilty, both at the same time. So Fergie had known all along that he was hiding something from him. Well, in a way this would make things easier. When he had recovered from his embarrassment, Johnny launched into a full explanation: He told about the "Saint Anthony" messages—Fergie giggled during this part—and then explained about the mysterious Mr. Finnick and his clock museum. Finally he explained how Father Higgins had figured out the meaning of one of the messages.

". . . and so we're gonna go out to Vinalhaven this Friday to see what we can find out," said Johnny, finishing up. He stared stubbornly and defiantly at Fergie. "Well, there's your big wonderful explanation," he added. "And if you think it's all so funny, you can stay home and wait to see if we bring the professor back with us. Okay?"

Fergie met Johnny's gaze. "I didn't think the whole thing was funny," he said with a straight face. "Just the part about leavin' notes under statues in churches in the middle of the night—I think that's a riot!"

Johnny was getting more irritated by the minute. "All right, all right, so it's a big fat laugh!" he snapped angrily. "I *knew* you'd make fun of the whole thing! That's why I never told you in the first place! You don't think we have a chance, do you?"

Fergie shrugged. "I dunno. Maybe you do, and maybe you don't. But all the same, I'd like to go along."

Johnny's mouth dropped open. He could hardly believe what he was hearing. Was Fergie kidding? "You wanta *what*?"

"I said, I wanta go along," replied Fergie calmly.

"Why? To make fun of us?"

Fergie shook his head. "Nope. I like trips, an' . . . an' I like goin' places with you. It'll be fun, like it was out at Scout camp. C'mon—let me go along. I promise I won't make fun of you guys. Cross my heart an' hope to die!"

Johnny was flabbergasted and confused as well. He really didn't know what to say. He was infuriated by Fergie's nerviness, and by his strange, confusing attitude toward the trip. But he really did want Fergie to go along. He enjoyed his company most of the time, and he had a hunch that he and Father Higgins might need an extra pair of hands. Fergie was a strong, sinewy, rugged kid. He looked gangly and awkward, but he could beat you at baseball or football or tug-of-war, and he could outrun a lot of the kids that Johnny knew. Johnny had no idea what they would be getting into out among those islands. They could use someone who could row a boat, or climb cliffs, or walk for hours without getting tired.

While Johnny mulled things over in his mind, he sat absolutely silent, staring at a point on the wall above Fergie's head. Fergie's eager grin quickly faded to a hurt frown. He wondered if maybe Johnny was thinking up some nice way of telling him to get lost.

"If you don't want me to come along, just say so!" muttered Fergie. He stabbed at the ice cream with his spoon and shoveled some into his mouth.

"Huh?" Johnny was jolted out of his trance, and in a flash he realized what Fergie was thinking. And he was genuinely touched. Fergie would feel crushed if he was left out. He wanted to be included because he liked trips. But he also wanted to be included because he was Johnny's best friend.

"I . . . I wasn't gonna tell you you couldn't come," said Johnny hastily. "It wasn't that, it was just that . . . well, Father Higgins is the one who's takin' me. He's runnin' the whole show. I was tryin' to figure out if maybe we could get him to take you too."

Fergie beamed, and Johnny felt glad. He really did want Fergie's company on this dangerous trip. But the question still remained: Could he persuade Father Higgins to include him?

"Oh, I think he'll take me along," said Fergie nonchalantly. He stared off into space and smiled secretively. "I mean, if it's up to him, I'm in like Flynn!"

Johnny blinked. "Why? Fergie, what in heck are you talkin' about?"

Fergie's grin got broader. "Oh, didn't I tell ya? I was the cleanup hitter on Father Higgins's City League softball team two years ago. That was before I knew you.

Higgy coaches kids' teams every summer. Well, that was the year that I broke up a no-hitter that some creep was throwin'. I got a triple in the ninth inning, an' Beaky Phelps brought me in with a single, an' we won the game. Didn't I ever tell you about any of that? Me'n Higgy're old buddies from way back!"

After Johnny had gotten over the shock of discovering that Fergie knew Father Higgins, he realized that this was going to be a much better trip than he had thought. Having two reliable friends along was a lot better than just having one. So Fergie and Johnny talked some more and tried to make plans, and then Johnny went home and called up Father Higgins. He knew right away from the way Father Higgins reacted that Fergie hadn't been kidding: the priest knew him and thought that he was a real character. In short, he liked him, and he'd be glad to take him along. First, though, he'd have to get the Fergusons' permission, and that would take a quick phone call and some sweet-talking. So Johnny hung up and paced around the living room.

Finally Father Higgins called back and said that Mrs. Ferguson had given them the go-ahead. Everything was set now. The three of them would be leaving on their journey around three P.M. on Friday. Father Higgins had been on a vacation trip to the Maine islands last year, and he figured that it would take them about three and a half hours of driving to get to Rockland, where they would catch the ferryboat that would take them to Vinalhaven.

The last ferry left at 7:32, so they would have an hour's leeway in case they got delayed. Since the ferryboat ride would take about an hour and a half, the three of them would arrive at the door of the Lobster Pot Inn on Vinalhaven at a little after nine.

It was a cloudy afternoon on Friday when Father Higgins's black Oldsmobile pulled up in front of the Dixon house on Fillmore Street. The horn beeped loudly, but there really was no need for this: Johnny was out on the front porch waiting, his suitcase in hand. Gramma and Grampa were with him. As Johnny watched, Father Higgins got out of the car, slammed the door, and waved at the three of them. He was wearing an open-necked plaid cotton shirt, baggy army fatigue trousers, combat boots, and an old army fatigue jacket. Stitched to the right shoulder of the jacket was a white cross, with a curved patch that said *Chaplain* above it. Johnny had never seen Father Higgins in his old sloppy weekend clothes before, but it was reassuring somehow —it made him seem more human and less stern and priestly and forbidding.

"Hi, there, John!" Father Higgins boomed as he walked toward them waving cheerily. "Are you ready for a voyage to the stern and rockbound coast of Maine and beyond?"

Johnny said yes, but his voice was weak and uncertain. Father Higgins was making it sound as if they were going to the moon. Also, he kept remembering the real purpose of this trip. In his stomach was a tight knot of fear.

Father Higgins saw how pale and tense Johnny looked, and he tried to cheer him up. "Oh, come on, John!" he said loudly as he took Johnny's suitcase from him. "You look like you were going to have your appendix out! This trip is going to be a lot of fun!"

Johnny tried to smile reassuringly. "It's . . . it's okay, Father," he said. "I . . . I always get nervous before I go on trips."

The priest smiled grimly, and in his eyes was a faraway look. "You do, eh? Well, you should try a trip where you're wading in a river with a lot of other soldiers in battle gear and helmets, while people on shore are firing mortar shells and machine-gun bullets at you. Now *there* would be something to be nervous about!"

Again Johnny was reminded that Father Higgins had been in some of the bloodiest battles of World War Two. He had been in the fighting on the Philippine Islands. He hardly ever talked about what had happened to him there, but Johnny got the feeling that he had seen some pretty awful things. And he also got the feeling that Father Higgins was a very courageous man. Johnny wanted to be courageous and bold, but he was having a tough time doing that right now. He told himself that this was a perfectly safe trip, that nothing bad could possibly happen to him. He was silly to be such a nervous nit.

So Johnny gave his grampa a hearty handshake, and he gave Gramma a big hug and a kiss.

"G'bye, John!" said Grampa. "Have a good time, an' bring us back a coupla shells off of the beaches!"

"God love ya, John!" said Gramma as her grandson hugged her tight. "Don't forget to wear your sweater when you go out at night. You don't wanta get strep throat or nothin' like that!"

Johnny turned and waved twice as he went down the walk with Father Higgins. Then the priest opened the trunk, threw in the suitcase, and slammed the lid. They both got into the car, the motor roared to life, and off they went. Their next stop was on Joy Street in Cranbrook, where Fergie lived. Father Higgins beeped his horn, and Fergie came racing out to the car to meet them, his suitcase in his hand. The outfit he was wearing was really something: he was all done up like a motorcycle thug. He had on skintight jeans and motorcycle boots and an amazing leather jacket that was all covered with spiky metal studs and colored glass reflectors. On the back was a picture of a big white skull with red glass reflectors for eyes. Over the skull were ragged white letters that spelled *Snake Eyes*.

Slam. That was the sound of Fergie's suitcase being pitched into the trunk of Father Higgins's car.

"Hi ho, Big John!" said Fergie jauntily as he slid into the wide front seat and slammed the car door. "How goes it, eh?"

Johnny said nothing. He was sitting stiff as a board, staring sightlessly at the windshield. All over his body he felt a ghastly, clammy, soul-numbing chill, a chill he could not explain. It had come over him when he saw the grinning red-eyed skull on the back of Fergie's jacket. Now, in his mind's eye, he saw a strange vision: It was as if he had X-ray eyes and was looking through the walls of his suitcase, which lay zipped and locked in the trunk of Father Higgins's car. Grinning up at him out of the dark, tiny and menacing, was the ivory skull.

CHAPTER SEVEN

Johnny clung to the rail of the gently pitching ferryboat as it plowed forward through the waters of Penobscot Bay. It was getting dark fast, and in the distance he saw the long white sweeping arm of a lighthouse beam. Even so, he could barely make out the vague shapes of islands, and out of the salt-smelling blackness came the dull *clank-clank* of a bell buoy as it rocked on the waves. In his ears throbbed the sound of the ferryboat's motor. It was a stubby little ship, with room for about four cars placed end to end. There were just two cars on this trip: Father Higgins's Oldsmobile and a station wagon that belonged to a lady who lived on the island. The cars stood end to end on the deck, with chocks under their wheels to keep them from moving. On the starboard and port sides of the little ship were small passenger cabins. Inside them were metal seats like the seats on buses, drinking fountains, and toilets. As far as Johnny knew, there was no one in the starboard-side cabin. Except for him all the passengers were in the other one. Johnny had been in there until a few minutes ago. He had been listening to Father Higgins play his guitar and sing Irish folk songs.

This trip had been a real eye-opener for Johnny: He had never realized that Father Higgins could be such a relaxed, life-of-the-party type. He had in his head an incredible collection of songs, mostly songs of the various Irish rebellions against the British crown. The songs were very stirring to Johnny, and when Father Higgins sang and played, he could almost see the lines of ill-clad pikemen marching up hills to do battle with the redcoats. Johnny had been in there with the rest for about an hour, but the fumes of Father Higgins's pipe had started making him dizzy, so he had finally gone out to get some air.

But he had also gone out for another reason. He had decided to do something about the tiny skull that he had stolen from the Childermass clock. All during the car trip Johnny had been haunted by the weird feeling that he had gotten when he saw the skull on Fergie's jacket. And he had finally decided that the skull was an evil thing, and that he'd better get rid of it. Earlier, he had made up a reason to borrow Father Higgins's car keys. He had opened the trunk of the Olds and dug out the watchcase with the skull inside it. Now the case was in the pocket of Johnny's raincoat. He could feel it pressing against his leg. But the time for action had come. After a quick look around, Johnny plunged his hand into the pocket. He pulled out the case and flipped it over the side. The boat's motor was roaring so loud that he did not even hear the splash.

Johnny heaved a sigh of relief. *That* was over with, anyway! It was possible, of course, that he had thrown away a good-luck charm, but . . .

A sound interrupted Johnny's thoughts—a clashing, banging noise. Johnny peered around through the gathering darkness, and then he saw it: The door on the empty cabin had come open, and it was hitting against the cabin's metal wall as the ship rolled, making a nerve-racking noise. Quickly he padded across the deck and grabbed the steel door handle. He was about to slam the door shut when he peered into the lighted cabin.

There was somebody . . . no, rather, it seemed to be some*thing* . . . sitting in one of the seats. It looked like a scarecrow. Its back was to Johnny, so he couldn't tell if it had a face, but it was wearing an odd sort of carroty red wig, and it was dressed in some sort of white coarse shirt. Johnny was puzzled. Why on earth would anyone bring a scarecrow onto a ferryboat? And just then, while he stood there wondering, the ship rolled gently, and the scarecrow lurched to one side. Johnny looked down, and he saw the scarecrow's foot sticking out into the aisle.

It was a skeleton foot. A cluster of white bones.

Johnny let out a bloodcurdling shriek. The door slipped from his hand and banged loudly as he reeled backward, spun around, took a few stumbling steps across the slippery steel deck, and clawed at the door of the other cabin. Somehow he found the handle and jerked the door open. Inside, he saw Father Higgins, Fergie, and the lady with the station wagon. They were all on their feet, staring, with their mouths open.

"Good God, John!" Father Higgins exclaimed. "What is it? Why did you yell like that?"

Johnny began a stammering explanation. He was having trouble putting words together, and he babbled something about a scarecrow with a skeleton inside it. "Come quick, please! Please, come and look!"

Father Higgins and Fergie glanced quickly at each other. Then the priest slipped the guitar strap over his head and laid the instrument down on the seat. With Fergie right behind him, he headed for the door.

"What is it?" gasped the woman, who had sunk back down into her seat. "What happened?"

"I don't know," muttered the priest grimly. "But I'm going to find out. You stay here, ma'am. We'll be right back."

Father Higgins and the two boys left the cabin and made their way across the deck to the cabin on the other side. The ferryboat was pitching and rolling more now, and the loose door clattered violently. Propping the door open with one brawny arm, Father Higgins stuck his head in through the doorway. Then he jerked his head back and peered questioningly at Johnny, who was standing behind him on the deck.

"Well?" rumbled Father Higgins. "Where is it? What did you do with it?"

Johnny was stunned. The priest was standing in the doorway of the cabin, and his large body blocked Johnny's view, and Fergie's as well. Johnny rushed forward and squeezed himself in beside Father Higgins to look. The cabin was empty. There was no sign of anyone, or anything on the seats.

Father Higgins turned slowly around and stared down at Johnny. He knew Johnny pretty well by this time, and he did not think Johnny was the kind of kid who would send people on a wild-goose chase just to get a laugh. Besides, Johnny did not look amused—he was ghostly pale. Clearly he had seen something. But what was it?

After a long, tense pause, Father Higgins cleared his throat. "Well! Gentlemen, let us be getting back to our seats."

Fergie and Johnny followed Father Higgins back to the other cabin. They went in and sat down and did not say a word, much to the annoyance of the lady passenger, who was expecting to hear that a murder victim had been found.

"Well? What is it? What did you find?" Her voice was high-pitched, almost hysterical.

"Nothing," said Father Higgins. There was an awful finality in his tone, and he glowered so threateningly that she was afraid to ask any more questions.

The four people in the cabin just sat there silently throughout the rest of the trip. Finally the ferryboat slowed, and Johnny could feel the boat backing into the dock. Putting his hand on the porthole rim, Johnny pulled himself up to look out. But it was so dark that he could hardly see anything at all.

"Come on, you two," said Father Higgins as he picked up his guitar and began to scoot sideways out of the seat. "We'd better be getting into the car. They'll be letting us drive off in a few minutes."

Johnny and Fergie followed Father Higgins out of the cabin, and they all climbed back into the big black Olds. With a shuddering, grinding sound the ferryboat eased itself into its berth between two rows of pilings. Ropes were passed around posts, and then the iron tailgate came clattering down. Father Higgins's car rolled onto the dock and down the winding two-lane road that led into the village of Vinalhaven. They drove down the main street of the picturesque little fishing town, took a sharp right onto a narrow dirt road, and before long they were pulling into the driveway of a small clapboard house that was next to a canal. The side porch of the house was built over the canal and stood on slime-coated pilings. A weathered signboard on the roof of the front porch said Lobster Pot Inn. In front of the sign, on the weathered shingles, lay a real lobster pot, which is a humped cage made of slats with a fishnet lining inside.

Johnny, Fergie, and Father Higgins lugged their suitcases inside, and the owner showed them to their rooms. After they had gotten washed up, they all sat down to a late supper of lobster rolls and cole slaw. The boys had cream soda to drink, and Father Higgins had a Budweiser. Johnny ate silently. His thoughts were on the scarecrow—or whatever it was—that he had seen and on the tiny skull that he had pitched overboard. He had seen the scarecrow right after he got rid of the skull—had he seen the scarecrow *because* he threw the skull away? *Oh well*, he thought wearily, *at least I got rid of the disgusting thing! If it's evil, it can go on being evil down on the bottom of the ocean. It won't bother me anymore.*

The next morning, at breakfast, Father Higgins talked with the boys about the second part of the Saint Anthony clue and his reasons for wanting to get inside Mr. Finnick's clock museum.

"As I told John here," Father Higgins said between sips of coffee, "the quotation 'a great reckoning in a little room' comes from Shakespeare's *As You Like It*. A 'reckoning,' in Shakespeare's time, meant a bill, like a restaurant bill, and the whole quote refers to a murder case that must've been the talk of London back in those days. The playwright Christopher Marlowe got stabbed to death in a drunken argument about a bill in a little bitty back room in a tavern. And now you're going to ask, 'What does this have to do with the professor's disappearance?' I don't know—not yet, anyway. But the 'little room' just *has* to be the little dollhouse room in that weird clock the professor's father made. The reckoning might be a miniature bill, and maybe on the back of it there's a map that'll lead us to where the professor's being held prisoner. All I know is, we've got to take our leads where we find them, so when you fellas finish stuffing your faces, we'll be off. Okay?"

Soon the three travelers had finished eating, so they hiked on over to Mr. Herman Finnick's clock museum. The museum turned out to be a large purple Victorian house covered with lacy iron trimmings and fancy wooden doodads. The house had just been freshly painted, and the lawn was carefully trimmed. A neat border of whitewashed rocks followed the sidewalk up to the ornate front door. Father Higgins stepped forward and pushed the door bell. After a short pause the heavy door rattled open, and there stood Mr. Fennick—short, sixty-ish, and prissy-looking, with a pencil-thin gray mustache and a disapproving frown on his face. He was wearing a blue denim apron, and in one hand he held a small can of all-purpose machine oil.

Mr. Finnick glanced at the boys and Father Higgins. He seemed a bit frightened, as if he expected them to leap at him and start pummeling him with their fists.

"Yes? What is it?" he snapped nervously.

Father Higgins stepped forward. "Hem! We've come to tour your clock museum, Mr. Finnick. We're especially interested in seeing . . ."

Mr. Finnick gave Father Higgins his sourest grimace. "Museum's not open till Memorial Day," he snapped. "Come back then, and I'll give you the complete tour." And he started to close the door.

But Father Higgins was not going to be shut out that easily. He put his large meaty hand on the door to keep it from closing. "I'm afraid there's been a misunderstanding," he said with a threatening hint in his voice and a glower on his face. "I'm the Father Thomas Higgins who wrote you from Duston Heights, Massachusetts, and asked if you'd give us a special tour. You said it'd be okay, don't you remember?"

A light dawned in Mr. Finnick's eyes, and a wintry thin smile creased his face. "Ah, yes. I remember now. You weren't wearing your clericals, so naturally I didn't —hrumph!—well, you understand. Please come this way. The tour fee is fifty cents apiece, by the way, payable in advance."

Mr. Finnick held out his thin, well-washed hand, and Father Higgins put a dollar and fifty cents into it. Then the three travelers followed the museum's owner into a vast entry hall that smelled of varnish, Roman Cleanser, and Murphy Oil Soap. The place was immaculate. The woodwork glistened, and the rugs had been freshly shampooed. Everywhere, on shelves and tables and hanging on the walls, were clocks. Tall ones, short ones, spring wound or weight driven. Seth Thomases and Waterbury eight-days and clocks made by all three of the Willard Brothers of Grafton, Massachusetts. Four grandfather clocks stood in a row by the foot of the main staircase—they looked like an overdignified and gloomy welcoming committee. The air was filled with a loud, chaotic storm of ticking, and as he ambled along through the rooms, Johnny couldn't help wondering if Mr. Finnick was annoyed by the fact that the clocks didn't all go *tick* and then *tock* at the same time. This thought made Johnny laugh suddenly, and Mr. Finnick turned and glanced at him unpleasantly.

"What's so funny, young man?" he rasped.

Johnny blushed. "It's, uh . . . it's nothing, sir. I . . . I just thought of a joke."

"Did you indeed?" said Mr. Finnick coldly. "Tell us, and then we all can laugh."

Father Higgins glowered down at Mr. Finnick. He was getting to like this fussy little man less and less. "Uh, Mr. Finnick?" he rumbled. "I wonder if we might see the Childermass clock. That's what we came here to see, after all. We're not especially, uh, clock fanciers, but my young friend John here has a friend who's a member of the Childermass family, and so this particular clock has sort of a . . . a sentimental meaning for him. You know what I mean?"

Mr. Finnick clasped his hands in front of him and cocked his head to one side. "Ah! A senti*mental* meaning!" he said in a nasty, mocking tone. "How nice! Well, now! The Childermass clock is a recent acquisition of mine, and I must say it is intriguing. Fine workmanship, and a real one-of-a-kind item. Very well. If you're bored with the rest of my clocks, I'll take you to see it without further delay. Please follow me."

Johnny, Fergie, and Father Higgins followed Mr. Finnick up a narrow back staircase. They came out on the second floor and walked down a long hall to the door of a room that had probably once been a bedroom. Inside were two large mahogany dining-room tables. One held a display case full of buttons, buttonhooks, pipe tampers, and glass paperweights. The other held the Childermass clock. It looked pretty much the way it had when Johnny saw it at the Fitzwilliam Inn, except that the woodwork was polished to a blinding luster, and the glass door over the face was spotlessly clean. Also, Mr. Finnick had set up a moveable glass-and-wood screen in front of the dollhouse-room part of the clock. Behind the screen the room's furniture was arranged as it had been when Johnny first saw the clock. But, amazingly, the oil lamp on the little oval table was lit! A pinpoint of flame flickered in the delicate glass chimney, and the lamp's yellowish light cast odd shadows over the rug, the bookshelves, and the tastefully papered walls. Quickly Johnny glanced at the row of shelves to the left of the fireplace. There, next to a bowl of tiny apples, was a gap—the space where the skull had been. There was even a tiny glue blob to mark the spot.

Mr. Finnick launched into a long, dull lecture that he must have memorized. Fergie and Father Higgins stood patiently listening with their arms folded, but Johnny kept darting suspicious glances at the little man. Just why had Mr. Finnick bought the clock, anyway? Was he mixed up in Professor Childermass's disappearance? Father Higgins thought that he was—at least, that was what he had said. But now that he had seen Mr. Finnick, Johnny found it hard to believe that this persnickety, irritable man had spirited the professor away by magic. Mr. Finnick did not look much like a wizard. On the other hand, the man might be concealing his true nature behind a mask. All right then, what if he *had* spirited the professor away? Why had he done it?

On droned Mr. Finnick. He was talking about double-foliot escapements and brass balance wheels. Suddenly Father Higgins tapped him on the shoulder—he had a request to make.

"Mr. Finnick? If you don't mind terribly, we'd like to see the inside of this little room up close. I wonder if you could move the screen and give us a little, you know, guided tour."

Mr. Finnick looked genuinely terrified. He seemed to be imagining the awful things that Fergie and Johnny might do with their big clumsy hands if he were to move the screen aside. But then he calmed down. He loved to lecture, and if the three visitors were willing to listen a bit more, he might make the supreme sacrifice.

"If you folks will just move back a teensy bit," said Mr. Finnick, waving them away with his hand. "Ah! Very good! Now, then!"

Johnny, Fergie, and Father Higgins stepped back a few paces. Then, carefully, Mr. Finnick set the screen aside. Taking a long, thin, spindly pair of tweezers from a pocket in his apron, he reached into the miniature room. Daintily he twisted a knob on the gas bracket on the wall. He showed how the drawer in the oval table could be made to slide out and in. He pulled a book out of the bookcase and laid it on the floor of the room. With the tweezer tips, he flipped a page or two to show that this was a real printed book. Mr. Finnick was a mine of information about furniture styles and fabrics and what ormolu really was. But as he rattled on, Johnny got more and more disappointed. He had hoped that a tiny replica of a bill would appear, stuck into a book. Or maybe it would be in the drawer of the oval table, or on the sideboard, or framed on the wall like a painting. But there wasn't anything that looked remotely like a bill. As Mr. Finnick lifted tiny umbrellas from the thimble-size umbrella stand and tweaked the frames of postage-stamp paintings with his tweezers, Johnny felt frustration and anger welling up inside him. They really were not finding out a thing.

Father Higgins scowled. He threw Johnny a sidelong glance, as if to say, *Looks like we lose, eh?* Johnny gave a little shrug. Father Higgins appeared to be fumbling about in his mind for some way to say good-bye. Finally, in the middle of one of Mr. Finnick's long sentences, the priest coughed loudly.

"Mr. Finnick," he said, glancing at his watch, "I am afraid we are going to have to be running along. We've got some other things that we have to do."

Mr. Finnick appeared to be deeply offended. He pulled the tweezers back, turned, and glared icily at the priest. "Am I to understand that you've had enough of my lecture?"

"I didn't say that," Father Higgins replied, with a smile. "I merely said that we'd have to be running along. Now do you suppose that you could show us the way out?"

Without another word, Mr. Finnick slid the glass screen back into place. Curtly, he motioned for the three visitors to follow him, and he led the way to the front door. In silence the glum little procession moved on down the hall and finally out to the front door. When they got there, Mr. Finnick jerked the door inward and stood stiffly at attention, like a dwarfish sentry.

"Good day to you all!" he mumbled, his lips barely moving. "Thank you for visiting the Finnick Clock Museum. Hmph. Hmph."

Father Higgins grinned and made a mock-courteous bow. At this, Mr. Finnick stepped back and slammed the door violently, making the glass pane rattle. Father Higgins shrugged and turned away. Then he and the two boys trotted on down the long walk and out onto a dirt road that wound past a weed-grown granite quarry. For a long while no one said anything. They just trudged along, eyes down. They had used one of the few leads that they had, and it had run them up against a blank wall. A wild idea went flitting through Johnny's head: Maybe they should break into the museum and *really* go over the dollhouse room, turn it inside out, and find the miniature bill or "reckoning" that the message had spoken of. And then Johnny wondered—not for the first time—if Mr. Finnick had been holding out on them. Had he been hiding the "great reckoning" on purpose? He sure didn't act like it. He had been stuffy, finicky, boring, and rude, but he hadn't acted secretive—not really. So where did that leave them all?

Father Higgins sighed loudly and discontentedly. He stooped, picked up a rock, and heaved it into the wilderness of granite blocks off to their right. "Well, boys!" he said. "We are not doing very well in the detection racket, are we?"

"Nope," said Fergie gloomily.

"I guess not," said Johnny, shoving his hands into his pockets. "What're we s'posed to do now? We're never gonna find the professor." Johnny's voice began to crack. He was fighting back the tears now. He had not felt so hopeless since this crazy business began.

Father Higgins stopped in the middle of the road. A few paces away, lying in a ditch, was a rough-hewn pillar of stone. It was covered with moss and lichens, but its top was flat, and so the priest walked over and sat down on it. Johnny and Fergie plumped themselves on the pillar too, and there was total silence for about three minutes.

"Well, gentlemen," said Father Higgins wearily, "it looks as if we have run up against a nice big solid stone wall. We didn't find out anything, did we? Not one single solitary useful fact or clue. However, we shouldn't despair, because—"

At this point Fergie interrupted him. "Whyn't we wait till dark an' then break in an' then turn that crazy clock upside down till we find some clues? I bet there's *somethin'* there—there has to be!"

Father Higgins shook his head. "I thought about breaking in, but it may be easier said than done. Finnick probably has the whole place wired with burglar alarms and electric eyes. But I do think we need to find out a bit more about our friend Finnick. Why don't we pay a trip to the Vinalhaven Public Library?"

Johnny was puzzled by this suggestion. "The library? How come?"

Father Higgins glanced at Johnny skeptically. "Oh, come on, John! For a scholarly kid you can be a bit thick sometimes! Finnick runs a museum, and so there will be articles about him in tourist guides and in books about the state of Maine and in back issues of newspapers. There may even be entries about him in reference books like *Who's Who in the East.* What we need to do is find something, anything, that will tie him in with magic or sorcery or Professor Childermass. After that we can decide whether or not it would be a good idea to do something drastic, like burglarizing his museum. So, off your duffs, me hearties! First we're going to go back to the inn so I can change into my clerical outfit—it may give me more authority, if I have to try to pry favors out of some nice sweet librarian. Then we're off to the library.

As I recall, it's not terribly far from the Main Street section of town. So, let's go! Time's a-wastin'!"

Fergie and Johnny did not think much of Father Higgins's plan, but they did not have a better one to offer, so they got up and followed him to the Lobster Pot Inn. When they got there, the boys waited around on the lawn outside while Father Higgins went to his room to change. In a short time he came back, and this time he was all done up in his black coat, black pants, glossy black shirtfront, and stiff white Roman collar. Down the road they hiked, till they came to the little cluster of shops and stores that was the business district of the island. At one end of the tiny Main Street was a stone watering trough, and a rutty cart track wound away from it up to the top of a grassy knoll. There, sitting all by itself, was a boxy gray one-story stone building.

"That's the library, boys," said Father Higgins, pointing. "It's probably not much, but it may have the answers we're looking for. Come on!"

Along the cart track they marched, single file, like a tiny army advancing against the enemy. On the steps of the library they halted, while Father Higgins brushed lint off his coat—he wanted to make himself as presentable as possible. Then, with Father Higgins in the lead, they trotted up the steps. Just inside the front door the little group stopped again. A few yards away, planted between two varnished golden oak pillars, was a desk. And behind it sat a small, elderly gray-haired woman. Her hair was done up into a bun, and a pencil was stuck into it. She had been reading a book, but now she looked up.

"Yes? What can I do for you?"

Father Higgins stepped forward with his hands folded in front of him. He said that he was writing a book about the Maine seacoast, and he would be grateful if the librarian could supply him with pamphlets and guide-books on the subject, and paper and pencil to take notes with.

The librarian led Father Higgins and the boys to the tiny reference room, which was not much more than a closet with bookshelves and a window. At a scarred wooden table the three of them sat down, and soon the librarian came in with a stack of books and pamphlets. All the rest of the morning they worked. They leafed busily through the material on the table. Every now and then someone would find a reference to Mr. Finnick's clock museum, and they would all stop and examine it. But they never found anything that seemed to be helpful.

At noon the weary researchers took a break for lunch, but an hour later they were back at their posts. As they ploughed through book after book, Johnny's spirits sank lower and lower. This was a crazy search. So far they had turned up absolutely nothing. Fergie was optimistic by nature, but even he was getting gloomy. Neverthe-less, Father Higgins struggled grimly on, his pipe clenched tightly in his teeth. All through the long after-noon they worked, taking occasional brief rest breaks to go outside and stretch their legs. The librarian popped in now and then to bring more books and to ask if she could help in any way.

Soon it was late afternoon. The sun was setting, and its long red slanting rays colored a patch on the wall behind Johnny's head. He was really going stir-crazy. He wanted to find the professor, but . . . well, he didn't care if he never saw another book as long as he lived.

"Father?" he said, breaking the busy silence. "Father? Can . . . can Fergie 'n' me go out for a little bit? I can't see straight anymore!"

Father Higgins smiled kindly. "Sure. You two go on out and walk around for a while. I'm gonna stay at this till dinnertime."

"Have . . . have you found anything?" asked Johnny falteringly.

Father Higgins's grim level gaze met Johnny's. "No," he said quietly. "But that doesn't mean I'm gonna give up. So run along, you two. I'll meet you at the inn for dinner."

Johnny and Fergie left the library and went out into the chilly evening air. The sun had just set, and the western sky was fringed with pale light. Down below, darkness was gathering.

"You know what?" said Fergie bitterly. "I feel like I've been pushin' a peanut up the road with my nose."

"So do I," muttered Johnny. "I just don't see what Father thinks he's gonna find. If old Finnick is a wizard . . . well, it wouldn't be in any guidebook, would it?"

Fergie put a stick of gum in his mouth and chewed it thoughtfully. "Higgy's a smart cookie, though," he said after a brief pause. "We wouldn't be doing all this work if he didn't have *some* kind of bright idea in the back of his head." Fergie scratched his nose. "John baby, I hate to mention this, but I need a bathroom. Wouldja mind waitin' here while I go back inside an' ask Mrs. Whatser-face where the little boys' room is?"

Johnny shook his head. It was a lovely evening. Venus was a glistening star hanging high in the west, and the damp, salt-tinged night air tasted good in Johnny's mouth. Whistling softly, he walked a few paces to the left on the dirt road that ran past the library steps. Behind the library, the road sank down into a shadowy hollow full of bushes and trees. Johnny decided that he would walk to the bottom of the hill and back again while he was waiting for Fergie. Down the hill he loped, still whistling. In the growing gloom Johnny could hardly see a thing, and he stumbled a few times over half-buried rocks. He was at the bottom now, and it was really pitch black. The trees and bushes seemed to crowd in around him. Twisting his head, he looked up at the library, a dark outline against the twilit sky. Not much to see down here, was there? Nothing but dark and weeds. Time to be getting back up to . . .

Johnny paused. Now that his eyes had gotten used to the dark, he saw something that he hadn't noticed before: a little house, an abandoned shanty, by the side of the road. The poor place had certainly seen better days: Its windows were broken, and the roof was half caved in. A crooked tree leaned against the side of the house, trailing its snaky branches over the bent chimney. *Gee*, thought Johnny, vaguely, *I wonder who lived in—*

And then two things happened with lightning suddenness. First Johnny felt a stinging cold spot against his thigh—it was as if a lump of ice had suddenly materialized in his pants pocket. Then a light appeared, a flickering orange glow that hovered over the dead leaves and matted grass outside the deserted house. In one window, behind the broken pane, a grinning jack-o'-lantern was burning.

CHAPTER EIGHT

Numb nightmare descended on Johnny. His scalp tingled, and he found it hard to breathe. In a flash he knew what the freezing lump in his pocket was—it was the skull, come back from a watery grave. Ahead of him the evil orange mask seemed to burn a hole in the night. It pulsated, sending out waves of power. Against his will, Johnny shuffled closer. Moving woodenly, like a robot, he clumped up the sagging steps and walked in through the dark doorway. A cobweb brushed his face, and he found that he could not raise his hand to brush it aside. He was in a shadowy room with a rotting plank floor. And he had barely time to wonder why there was no pumpkin in the room when a violent blow brought him to his knees. A ghastly, impossibly huge jack-o'-lantern face appeared spread across one wall of the room. It was throbbing, and the air around Johnny heaved to an insane, feverish rhythm. His chest felt tight, and his eyesight was clouded by an icy mist that wrapped itself around him. Johnny struggled for breath—the life was being pumped out of him. He was going to die. Suddenly a voice burst in on his brain, a harsh, grating, stony voice that told him he would never again meddle in things beyond his understanding. *Death is an eternal sleep*, said the voice, and it said this over and over like a cracked record. Desperately Johnny fought to stay alive, but he knew that he was losing—he was starting to black out. Just before he lost consciousness, he heard something—a commotion in the room. A door slammed, and somebody shouted strange words, words that sounded like *Lumps and crust!* The voice rang out two or three times. And then Johnny was gone.

When he woke up, he was lying on the damp grass outside the old shack. Fergie was kneeling beside him, and Father Higgins was standing over him, looking very huge and forbidding in spite of the friendly smile on his face. In his large hairy hand the priest was holding a small silver crucifix on a chain.

"Wha . . . wha . . ." muttered Johnny thickly. He felt limp and woozy, as if he had just recovered from the flu. With an effort he raised his head and glanced toward the old shack. It was dark, lost in the evening shadows.

Then a sudden stab of terror hit him, and he fumbled at his thigh. It was gone—the skull, the thing that had suddenly appeared in his pocket—it had vanished.

Johnny turned his head and looked at Fergie. "Did . . . did you take it?" he asked in a quavering voice.

Fergie looked puzzled. "Take what, John baby? I dunno what you're talkin' about."

With an effort Johnny forced himself to sit up. As he did this, Father Higgins sank to his knees beside him. He still clutched the crucifix, and he held it up as if he were using it to ward off an attacker. With his other hand he tried to gently force Johnny to lie back down on the ground.

"Easy, John, easy!" said the priest softly. "You've been through something awful, and you're probably still weak. The powers of darkness were here, and they were after you. You need some rest."

But Johnny shook off the priest's hand. He was feeling better by the minute. "Father," he said, pointing toward the dark house, "did . . . did you see it?"

Father Higgins looked grim. "If you mean that Halloween face, yes, I saw it. I saw it from way up at the top o' the hill, where I was talkin' with young Byron here. He was tryin' to figure out where you had gone to, and then all of a sudden I saw that face, and I remembered what you had told me. So I charged on down the hill and busted into that house over there, and all of a sudden I was face to face with that horrible thing on the wall, and I felt the presence of evil all over my body. I don't mind tellin' you, I nearly turned and ran. But I pulled myself together, and then I gave the rotten, miserable thing a good dose of *this*!" He held up the crucifix and shook it menacingly. "This's a blessed crucifix, and there's this glass bubble on it, and underneath are two splinters from the True Cross, the cross Jesus was crucified on. And I said *lumen Christi*, which means *light of Christ*. It's a powerful charm and part of the Holy Saturday service. Y'see . . ."

Johnny laid his hand on the priest's arm. "Father," he said nervously, "I . . . I have to tell you something."

Father Higgins grinned. "I'll just bet you do. Well, go ahead. I'm listening."

Johnny began slowly, with lots of little stops and starts. As clearly as he could, he explained about the skull. He told how he had found it, how he had felt when he owned it, and why he had finally decided to get rid of it. He also described the strange vision that he had had in the workroom of the Fitzwilliam Inn at midnight. This was the first time that Johnny had been able to tell anyone about these things, and it felt wonderful to just get everything off his chest.

"How . . . how come I couldn't talk about this before?" he asked, staring hard at the priest. "I couldn't tell the professor. Every time I tried I got this awful pain in my chest, and I felt like I couldn't breathe. Why couldn't I tell him?"

"John," said Father Higgins slowly and gravely, "it is becoming more and more clear to me that we are dealing with some kind of incredibly evil intelligence, a disembodied spirit that has decided to attack you and the professor for some reason. The skull and the jack-o'-lantern face and the scarecrow you saw on the ferryboat —they are all manifestations of that evil mind. Well, the mind did not want you to tip off the prof that something bad was going to happen to him. It also did not want you to do anything that might clear up the mystery of the prof's disappearance. And do you want to know why you can tell us now? The evil influence was driven off by the power of the True Cross. You feel better now, don't you—getting the thing out in the open, I mean."

Johnny nodded. "Yeah, I do. Do you think that vision I saw at the Fitzwilliam Inn has anything to do with the second clue, the one about the great reckoning in the little room? I should've thought of this before, but it just wasn't clear to me. What I'm tryin' to say is, the room in the vision is the little room, the dollhouse room—only full size."

Father Higgins patted Johnny on the shoulder. "Very good, my friend! Very *good*! And a reckoning is the settling of an account—that is one meaning of the word, anyway—and it certainly looks like you saw a reenactment of the way the professor's granduncle got *his* account settled! Hmmm. Things are getting clearer. Not a whole lot clearer, but somewhat clearer. I wish we knew more about the skull that you took from the dollhouse room. If we knew why the prof's father chose to put it in the—"

"Will it come back?" Johnny blurted suddenly. He sounded very anxious. "That is, it . . . it came back once, so it must be able to come back whenever it wants to. How . . . how'm I gonna get rid of it?"

"I don't know, John," said Father Higgins. He bit his lip and glared into the night. "I wish I knew more about what's goin' on, but I don't. However, I do know this. My crucifix saved you, and so you better keep it for the time being. Here."

Father Higgins pressed the crucifix into Johnny's hand. "There's a chain on it," he went on. "Put it around your neck, and don't take it off for *any* reason! You understand?"

Johnny nodded and smiled gratefully. He looped the chain around his neck and slid the crucifix in under his shirt, but just as he had finished doing this, he turned his head and noticed something. Fergie was gone!

"Hey, Father!" he exclaimed, looking about wildly. "What happened to Fergie?"

With a loud exclamation Father Higgins sprang to his feet. He turned just in time to see Fergie appear out of the darkness. He was coming from the direction of the shack, and he was holding something in his hands.

Father Higgins's jaw sagged. Then he got angry. "Byron!" he roared. "What the devil do you think you're doing?"

Fergie smiled sheepishly and shrugged. "I . . . uh, I just thought I'd like to go an' see what the old place was like. Just to see, y'know."

Father Higgins was stunned. "Good grief, man! Do you realize what that house *is?* It's a den of Satan! Don't you have any sense at all? And what, in the name of heaven, is that thing you've got in your hands?"

Fergie held the thing out, and now Johnny saw that he had in his hands an old leather-bound book with dog-eared covers. It looked very dirty, and a long piece of cobweb trailed from one end of it. With a look of awe and fear on his face, Father Higgins reached into the inner pocket of his jacket and took out a Pen-Lite. He snapped it on and played the narrow beam over the cover of the book. In a gingerly way he took hold of the cover and folded it back. Curious, Johnny scrambled to his feet and joined the other two, who were huddled over the book, peering at the flyleaf. Now Johnny saw that there was old-fashioned writing with lots of odd loops and flowing swirls on the moldy, liver-spotted sheet. But it was not hard to read. It said:

> *Warren Windrow*
> *A great reckoning in a little room—*
> *this I dreamt, April 30, 1842.*

"Well, I'll be darned!" exclaimed Father Higgins. With an odd expression on his face, he reached out and carefully peeled back the flyleaf. Now they were looking at the title page. At the top, large black letters said *La Clavicule de Salomon.* Under this title was a crude engraving of a leering demon's face inside a circle, and around the outside of the circle the word *Azoth* was repeated over and over. Father Higgins wrinkled up his nose, as if he were smelling something unpleasant. As Fergie held the book steady for him, the priest riffled quickly through several pages.

"This is a book of black magic," he said, looking up at last. "It's printed in French, and my French isn't terribly good, but I can make out enough to tell what's being said. Now . . ."

Then something happened. Johnny reached out and—for the first time—actually touched the book, which began to steam and smoke. With a loud yell, Fergie dropped it, and the other two leaped back. The pages of the book began to writhe and twist, and more whitish smoke curled upward. It was burning—being consumed by a fire that could not be seen. In a few minutes there was nothing left on the ground but a heap of gray ashes.

"Angels and ministers of grace defend us!" breathed Father Higgins as he crossed himself.

"What . . . I mean, how come . . ." stammered Johnny in confusion.

"You were wearing the silver cross," said Father Higgins solemnly. "And you touched the cursed thing, and so it was destroyed." He heaved a deep sigh and turned to Fergie. "Byron, I don't know what crazy—or blessed —force it was that drove you to go into that house and bring that book out, but you have given us our first good lead. Warren Windrow . . . hmm. I wonder who he was, and why he dreamed the same phrase that was given to us by the mysterious writing that we found under the statue. Well, come on, gentlemen. We're going back up to the library. John? Are you able to navigate okay?"

Johnny nodded. Most of the queasiness and dizziness had worn off, and he felt more like himself again. With Fergie on one side of him and Father Higgins on the other, he climbed the hill once more. Above them the windows of the library glowed yellow, and all around the trees rustled in the night breeze that had suddenly sprung up. When they reached the front steps of the library, Father Higgins told the boys to wait outside. He said that he had a pretty good idea of the kind of book he wanted to look for, and he wouldn't be long. So Fergie and Johnny sat down on the granite steps and waited. They watched the stars and listened to the shrill piping of May frogs in some nearby pool. Finally Father Higgins returned. And from the way he was grinning and rubbing his hands together, they knew he had found something.

"Hey, Father, what is it?" asked Fergie as he scrambled to his feet. "Didja find out who that guy was?"

"I did indeed!" exclaimed the priest, who was practically bubbling over with self-satisfaction and triumphant glee. "Yes, I most certainly did! Come along, gentlemen, and I'll tell you everything."

Father Higgins started walking toward a clump of dark shadowy trees that rose on the horizon.

"Hey, Father!" exclaimed Johnny, running after him. "The inn's back that way!"

"Yes, I know it is," said Father Higgins as he strode

along. "But we aren't going to the inn. We're going down to the beach, to a boathouse run by a guy named Hank Dodge. When I was out here last year, I rented a boat from him, and I think I'm gonna do it again. He also sells camping supplies and canned food to dumb landlubbers like us who come out here without being prepared to go on an expedition."

Johnny's mouth dropped open. "Expedition? Father, where are we going?"

"Yeah, come on, Father!" added Fergie, who was walking on the other side of him. "Give us the whole story!"

For a few minutes Father Higgins walked on in silence. The boys found that they were on a winding blacktop road, and the tarred surface felt hard now after the spongy earth they had been treading on. At last Father Higgins was ready to talk. He took a deep breath and began to explain that he had had to leaf through three books of old New England legends before he found the story he was looking for. It was in a book called *Weird Tales of the Maine Seacoast* and told the saga of a man named Warren Windrow, whose ghost supposedly had been seen quite a few times on Vinalhaven and on some of the nearby islands. Back in the 1840s he had lived on Cemetery Island, which was just a dot on the map out in Hurricane Sound, not far from Vinalhaven. Windrow had come from a large family that once lived in the Penobscot Bay area, and the family had a sinister reputation, though the book didn't say why.

Well, one day Warren Windrow caught the California gold fever that was sweeping the eastern half of the country in those days, and he went out to California to see if he could strike it rich. Windrow didn't find any gold, but he did get into a saloon fight with another Easterner—a man from Vermont, a man named Lucius J. Childermass. Windrow got beaten up, and apparently he decided to get even, because one night—some time after the fight—he jumped Lucius in a dark alley and tried to kill him with a Bowie knife. Lucius got cut up a bit, but some people who were passing in the street nearby broke up the fight and rescued Lucius. Windrow was taken to San Francisco, where he was tried for attempted murder, convicted, and hanged.

". . . and that's the whole story, as far as I can get it from the book I read," said Father Higgins, finishing up. "So we have the ghostly Warren Windrow, and a book of black magic that he once owned, and a tale that connects him with the professor's granduncle. This is all beginning to make sense, in a weird way. Our next step will be to go and have a little look at Cemetery Island. It's not far, only about half an hour's ride. I know Byron here is rarin' to go, but I thought I'd better ask you if you wanted to stay behind, John. You can wait for us, and no one will think you're cowardly or anything like that. And for all I know, we may not find anything but sand and seashells. We ought to be back pretty quick, in any case. What d'ye say, John?"

Johnny squared his jaw and looked as determined as

he possibly could. He was still feeling a bit shaky because of the ghastly experience he had just had, but he wasn't going to be cheated out of an adventure. Besides, the professor was more his friend than he was anybody else's—or so he felt, anyway.

"I wanta go, Father," he said defiantly. "You'll hafta tie me up an' chain me to a tree if you want me to stay here."

The road they took petered out into a sandy track that wound over some grassy hummocks and past a long narrow pond that glimmered in the starlight. Before long they arrived at a little cove with a few houses clustered around its edges. At the end of a row of white clapboard shanties stood the Old Harbor Boathouse, a big sprawling building with cedar shingles and a slate roof. Next to the boathouse was a little poky building with a sagging roof and a metal stove chimney. A sign that leaned against the house gave the name of the establishment and listed the rental rates and the name of the owner in straggling white letters: *Hank Dodge, prop.*

Father Higgins knocked loudly on the door of the house, and Hank Dodge came out. He wore saggy blue work pants, a red-and-white hunting jacket, and a fishing hat stuck full of fishing flies. His face was red-veined and jowly, and his breath smelled of whiskey. Father Higgins told him what he wanted and pressed a wad of bills into his hand. While waiting for Hank to return, Father Higgins made up a list in his head and rattled it off to Fergie: a couple of cans of beans, a mess kit, a can of Sterno, matches, a tarpaulin, three flashlights, and a bottle of brandy. Fergie recited this list again, took some money from Father Higgins, and raced off down the beach toward a lighted store that he saw in the distance. Hank Dodge returned with the keys to the boat and an oil lantern and led Johnny and Father Higgins around to the back door of the boathouse.

A few minutes later, Fergie, Johnny, and Father Higgins were skimming along over a body of water known as Hurricane Sound. Off to their left, in the distance, rose the low, humped shape of Hurricane Island. Overhead a few stars could be seen through a filmy, overcast sky, and from out in the direction of the open sea came ominous rumbles and occasional lightning flashes—a storm was moving into the mouth of the bay. Johnny sat in the bow seat. He clung tightly to the sides of the boat and felt absolutely petrified—motorboat rides had always scared the dickens out of him. Fergie sat in the middle seat, arms folded and a calm expression on his face, and in the stern sat Father Higgins. He chewed at his empty pipe and maneuvered the steering handle of the motor. Out toward the entrance of the Sound they shot, a long white wake spewing behind them and a loud engine drone filling the air. They were on their way— toward what?

Johnny could not for the life of him imagine how all this was going to end. But as he sat there with the motorboat hurtling along under him, he knew that he was getting more nervous by the minute. Part of this was because of his fear of riding in a speeding boat, but there was more to it than that. Johnny kept thinking of the skull—he couldn't keep his mind off it. The grinning evil, little object was gone again—it had vanished back into the void, where dark things wait, until witchcraft calls them forth. Without a doubt the silver crucifix had driven the skull away—but could it *keep* the skull away? What if the skull reappeared at some time, when he least expected it? Johnny brooded about the skull. He closed his eyes and wished fervently that he had never heard of the Childermass clock, or Cemetery Island, or Penobscot Bay.

"There it is!" Fergie yelled, pointing into the darkness ahead.

Johnny forced his eyes open and twisted his head around. Looming closer and closer was a dark shadowy mass. He couldn't make out any details—it was pitch black out here in the middle of the bay. The drone of the motor grew softer as Father Higgins aimed the boat in toward the shore. Then the engine noise died altogether, and they coasted in. Johnny felt a rough shudder and heard a grumbling of sand under his feet. They had landed.

Awkwardly the tall priest stood up and swung himself out of the boat. He was calf-deep in water, but he didn't seem to mind. Fergie leaped nimbly out and began tugging at the gunwales of the boat. But then he noticed that Johnny was still sitting there, rigidly staring at nothing.

For a second Fergie looked worried, but then he grinned, reached up, and slapped Johnny hard on the knee. "Hey, Dixon!" he said loudly. "Off your duff and on your feet! How're we gonna drag the boat in if you sit there weighin' it down? Come on! Afraid to get your feet wet? Your gramma tell you you'd catch cold if your toesies got damp?"

Fergie was being nasty and sarcastic on purpose. He was a bit scared of the way Johnny was acting, and he figured that it might be best to jolt him into action.

"Huh? Oh . . . oh, yeah," muttered Johnny in a dazed, thick voice. He lurched to his feet and clambered over the side of the rowboat. The icy cold of the water gripped his legs, and he winced. But he bit his lip to keep from yelling—he wanted to prove that he was just as tough as the other two. Moving to the front of the boat, he gripped the iron ring that hung from the prow, and he tugged. The others were shoving too, and the boat slid up onto the gravelly beach.

They walked a few steps over the wet sand and then stopped to stare at the island. Pine trees grew close to the shore, and beyond rose shelves of granite. The wind was picking up now, and the pines waved to and fro, making an eerie keening noise. Then lightning flashed again in the distance, and Father Higgins swore under his breath.

"We're gonna get rained on, gentlemen!" he growled. "I'm kinda glad I thought of that tarpaulin—we might just possibly be in need of it." He turned, put his hands on his hips, and peered into the murky shadows of the island. "Well, prof," he said loudly, "I sure hope you're here! Comin', ready or not, like us kids used to say!"

After this little speech Father Higgins turned abruptly, went back to the boat, and fumbled under the tarpaulin. He came up with the three flashlights, and with a jaunty flick of his wrist, he sent one flying into Fergie's outstretched hands. Johnny caught the other one.

"I wonder if we ought to've brought our raincoats," said Johnny fretfully as he switched on his light. He had a fear of dampness, and he was always fussing about it. Fergie snickered, and Johnny bit his lip ruefully. Why did he say things like that? Like most timid people, Johnny wanted to be brave and resourceful and cunning. Why couldn't he just shrug off fears the way other people did? Then he reminded himself that he was here on the island, after all, with the other two. So maybe he wasn't quite as cowardly as he thought he was.

With flashlights shining, Fergie, Johnny, and Father Higgins tramped up the beach and plunged into the scrubby little clump of pines. They found a narrow winding path that was covered with dead pine needles and decided to follow it. On the other side of the pine grove, the rugged uneven ground of the island opened out before them. It was too dark to see much, but here and there were dark blotches that might be bushes. And there were rocks—Johnny kept tripping over them as he picked his way along. The three of them marched on in silence for some time while the wind whistled around them, and big splatting raindrops started to fall. Suddenly Father Higgins let out an exclamation.

"Hey! Wouldja look at that? Up there!"

Johnny and Fergie looked. Far ahead, in the darkness, was a tiny yellow blot of light. A lamp in a window, maybe.

"Come on, boys!" yelled Father Higgins, waving them ahead excitedly. "This miserable little hunk of real estate isn't supposed to have anybody living on it. But where there's light, there's life, or so they say. Let's go see!"

The three of them walked faster now. Fergie and Father Higgins swung right along—they did not seem to be having any trouble with the uneven stony field. But it was another story for Johnny: He banged his shin on a tree stump, and a little later he stepped into a hole that gave his ankle a vicious twist.

"*Ow!*" yelled Johnny as his foot sank into the hole. "That hurts, it *hurts!*"

Father Higgins and Fergie were a few paces ahead of him. They stopped and turned their flashlight beams on their friend.

"Hey, John!" Fergie called. "Are you okay?"

Johnny did not reply immediately. He yanked his foot out of the hole. Then he took a careful, gingerly step— and sucked in his breath with a sharp, painful hiss. It was agony to walk. Gritting his teeth, he forced himself to take another step. The second step felt just as miserable as the first had, but at least he could move. Hobbling, he made it up to where the other two were standing.

Father Higgins laid his hand on Johnny's arm. "How are you, John? What does it feel like?"

Johnny forced himself to stare straight into the priest's eyes. "It's . . . it's okay," he said in a strained voice. This, of course, was a lie. His ankle felt as if somebody were toasting it over a bonfire. But he wasn't going to be left out of the search. A long time ago somebody had told him that your ankle wasn't broken if you could still walk. Well, he could walk. That was all that mattered, for now.

"You sure you're all right?" asked Father Higgins. He sounded worried.

"I'm fine, Father. It . . . it hurts a little, but not much."

Father Higgins gave Johnny a friendly pat on the back. "Okay, then—we're off! Forward at the gallop, as they say in the cavalry movies!"

The three of them tramped on. The long white beams of their flashlights picked out a low fieldstone wall, and behind it long rows of pale white slabs that marched up a hillside—the graveyard for which Cemetery Island was named. Beyond the wall the ground rose steadily. Johnny could see a rutty little road rising into the darkness. At the top was the shadow of a building—a chapel maybe. And there was the lighted window. As Johnny watched, a shadow passed before the light. Somebody was in there, moving around!

"Holy Saint Patrick!" whispered Father Higgins in an

awestruck voice. "I wonder if . . . Well, come on! What're we waiting for?"

At the entrance to the cemetery was a rusting iron turnstile. It creaked and squealed loudly as the three of them shoved through it. Hobbling badly now, feeling agony in every step and sweat streaming down his face, Johnny struggled to keep up with his friends. Up the road they ran. As they got nearer to the top, they could see that the building was indeed a chapel, a tiny brick church with quatrefoil decorations on the front and a pointed door with a cross over it. One of the long, narrow windows was boarded up, but the other was open, and light was streaming out of it. Father Higgins got to the door first. He jerked it open, and a bar of light fell across the road. Then the priest took a step backward and just stood there, dead still. Johnny and Fergie crowded in next to him to look.

The inside of the little chapel was a mess. Wooden pews were stacked in a corner, and everything seemed to be covered with gritty dust and dirt. The altar at the rear had been used as a dinner table: a checkered tablecloth was thrown over it, and on it lay a dirty plate with a half-eaten piece of bread and a battered tin cup. Near the cup and plate stood an oil lamp that cast a yellowish smoky light. A few paces from the altar stood an old-fashioned iron cookstove, and in one corner was a dirty striped mattress with an old threadbare blanket wadded up on it and a rust-stained pillow with no pillowcase. Pulled up near the stove was a rickety, cane-bottomed rocking chair, and in it sat a little old man. He wore a very soiled and wrinkly white shirt and a scubby brown sweater with egg stains on it. His pants were coated with floury patches of white dust, and the upper parts of his shoes were starting to separate from the soles. You could see his toes through the holes—he wasn't wearing socks. On the old man's head was a wild mess of white hair with bits of twigs in it. His sideburns needed trimming, and his face was smudged with dirt. Perched askew on the man's reddish nose was a pair of rimless spectacles. His fingernails were broken and dirty, and he was clutching a tattered newspaper. Professor Childermass looked up at the priest and the two boys who were standing in the doorway.

"Well?" he snapped crankily, leaning forward to squint at the three intruders. "Who are you, and what do you want? I don't like people bursting into my house without knocking. I asked you a question, and I expect an answer! *What the devil do you want?*"

CHAPTER NINE

The professor leaned forward, waiting for a reply. But his visitors were too astonished to answer. Johnny and Fergie looked at each other, and they both glanced helplessly at Father Higgins, who was just standing there with his mouth open. After an awkward silence Father Higgins spoke. He sounded wary and uncertain, as if he really didn't know what would be best to say.

"Rod? Rod, don't you recognize us? It's me, Father Higgins, from St. Michael's church. And here's your old pal, Johnny, and his friend Fergie. We've been turning the countryside upside down looking for you, and we're so glad we've found you! Come on! Do . . . do you *really* not know who we are?"

The professor went on glaring suspiciously at his

visitors. "I can see that you're a priest," he said sullenly. "Or rather, I see that you're wearing a clerical outfit. But I can honestly say that I've never met you before in my life. And the same goes for those two disreputable-looking kids you've got with you. Now, if you don't mind, I'd like you to go away and leave me in peace. Today's my birthday, and tonight—if I'm good—something especially nice is going to happen to me. I wouldn't want to miss out on *that* now, would I? So please make yourselves scarce, the lot of you!"

Again Johnny was stunned. Stunned and horrified. Not only had the professor lost his memory, but he also seemed to be slightly insane. Johnny knew very well when the professor's birthday was: December 8. And what was this "something special" that was going to happen to him?

Father Higgins took a short step forward. He clenched and unclenched his fists, and he looked grim and threatening. But when he spoke, his voice was gentle and kindly.

"Sir? Is it possible that you're really not good old Rod Childermass? I mean, we may have come to the wrong house by mistake, in which case I beg your pardon. But you looked so much like Rod Childermass that . . . Well, would you mind telling us your name?"

The professor seemed a bit taken aback by this question. He put his fingers to his lips and pondered for a bit. "You know," he said in a sincere, matter-of-fact tone, "I can't honestly say *who* I am! But names aren't important, are they? They're like the labels on jars, and they may be misleading. On the other hand, I can tell you a great deal about history. I can tell you about the War of the Spanish Succession, and the Zimmermann Telegram, and the Ostend Manifesto. Would you care to hear a few words about these subjects? Ask me anything, anything at all!"

Tears sprang to Johnny's eyes. He felt utterly helpless and panicky too. If they had found the professor chained to a wall, they could have broken the chains and led him away to safety. But in the state he was in, it would be hard to get him to go away with them peacefully. Johnny threw a quick glance at Father Higgins, who loomed up in the doorway, big and strong. Every muscle in the priest's body seemed tense, and a wild thought leaped into Johnny's head: Would Father Higgins try to take the professor away by force? In his mind's eye Johnny saw the priest swooping down on the little old man and throwing him over his shoulder like a sack of potatoes. Johnny waited, and it seemed as if Father Higgins were gathering himself for a leap. But then he relaxed, stepped back, and turned to the boys.

"Come on, kids," he said softly, turning and putting his hand on Johnny's shoulder. "It's clear that this gentleman wants to be left alone. Let's clear out."

Reluctantly Johnny and Fergie let Father Higgins push them out the chapel door in front of him. When they were all outside, the priest gripped the iron ring on the door and pulled it shut. He squinted grouchily at the falling rain, and then he turned to the boys.

"Gentlemen," he said in a quiet, confidential tone, "we have got a problem on our hands. Something has clearly happened to the prof. Maybe he hit his head, or maybe some kind of evil sorcery is at work. At any rate, he won't budge. What the dickens do you think we ought to do?"

Fergie said what Johnny was thinking. "I think you oughta go in there and put a half nelson on him and drag him away. I mean, he's outa his jug, and that is just about the only way you're gonna get him to come, Father. Anyways, you're bigger'n he is, an' I don't think he'd give you too much of a fight."

Father Higgins rubbed his chin and pondered. "Hmm . . . you may be right, Byron. On the other hand, the prof is tougher than he looks. He works out with dumbbells, and he walks several miles a day. I could pin him down, but it'd be a real job draggin' him away. He told me once he learned to fight dirty in his college wrestling classes, and if he remembers any of his nasty little tricks . . . well, you might have a crippled priest on your hands, and no professor. And anyway, I don't feel right about hitting him—he's my friend, out of his mind or not."

"So what're we gonna do?" asked Fergie irritably. "Do we just stand around out here an' twiddle our thumbs while we wait for the prof to get his marbles back? That seems kinda dumb to me."

"Yes, dumb it would be," muttered Father Higgins. "However, I have a plan in mind: Do you remember that bottle of brandy I had you buy? Well, why don't you two wait here and make sure that our friend doesn't wander away, and I'll scoot back to the boat and get the brandy. It's Hennessy Five Star, and if he still has any of his old taste buds left, he'll *love* it! And once I've managed to pour enough of the old sauce into him, it ought to be a fairly simple matter to get our old pal into the boat and out of this miserable place. Whaddaya say, guys? Sound like a good plan?"

Fergie and Johnny nodded in agreement. Quickly the priest went barreling down the little cemetery road and vaulted over the turnstile with surprising agility. Then his bulky form was swallowed up by the dark, rainy night.

Fergie stood solemnly watching him go, his arms folded. "Boy, I sure hope he'll be all right!" he said with feeling.

Johnny turned to him, alarmed. "Why'd you say that, Fergie? I mean, what . . . whaddaya think could happen?"

Fergie shrugged gloomily. "I dunno. But this is all gettin' to be a pretty weird business, and I keep thinkin' that *anything* is liable to happen! There's that run-in you had down behind the library, for instance. And here's the prof, sittin' in there not knowin' who he is. And there's that skull that you said came back and showed up in your pocket after you threw it away. So like I said, I get the feelin' that the mullygrubs might come and get us any second now." Fergie laughed nervously. He shivered in the drizzle and buttoned the top button of his leather jacket. "By the way," he went on, "what was all that about it bein' the prof's birthday? It isn't, is it?"

Johnny shook his head. "Nope, it sure isn't! I dunno *what* he said that for! But what worries me is, he acts like he's waitin' for somethin' to happen. Whatever it is, I sure hope it doesn't happen till we get him away from here!"

Fergie glanced at the closed chapel door. "I hope we can get him away. Period!" he said, and he bit his lip nervously.

The wind began to blow harder. An old bent elm tree grew in the field that lay beyond the graveyard wall, and they could see it waving its spindly, loopy arms. As the rain poured down, the boys squeezed themselves in against the chapel wall. There was no porch, but the edge of the roof hung out a little over the front of the building, and this kept them a bit drier than they would have been otherwise. Time passed. Every now and then Johnny would glance to his right, at the pool of lamplight that lay on the gravel outside the open window. There was no glass in the window, so he could hear the professor stirring around inside. He heard him sniffle and cough and get up and shuffle around. Then the professor went back and sat in the rocker, which creaked noisily as he moved to and fro. Johnny wanted very much to hammer on the door and demand that the professor let them in. But somehow it seemed wiser to stay outside, even though the rain was giving him and Fergie a good soaking. If the professor's mind was unbalanced, Johnny didn't want to do anything that would push him over the edge into total, screaming madness. Better to wait for Father Higgins to show up with his bottle of Hennessy Five Star. But the minutes ticked on, and Father Higgins did not come back. Johnny switched on his flashlight and peered at his watch, which said five after nine. He wasn't sure when the priest had left, but it seemed like it was an hour ago. Johnny was soaked to the skin, and his sprained ankle burned like fury. And on top of everything else, the chill had gotten into his bones. When he opened his mouth to speak, he found that his teeth were chattering.

"F-Fergie," he stammered, "wh-where do you think F-Father H-Higgins has go-gone to?"

"You got me. He's had enough time to go back to Duston Heights by now. I'm worried, John baby. I think one of us oughta go down to the boat and check up. You wanta do it?"

Johnny grimaced and shook his head. "I better not. I sprained my ankle real bad while we were runnin' across that field out there, an' it's all swelled up now. I think I might faint if I tried to run."

Fergie looked at him in astonishment. "Oh, great! Just great! I thought you said you were okay after you stepped in that hole! Why didn't you tell us about this before, for God's sake?"

"I didn't want you guys to make me go back," said Johnny miserably. "And anyway, I thought it might get better. But it hasn't—it feels awful!"

Fergie groaned. He stared helplessly up at the rain. "Well, then, I guess I better go!" he said, heaving a disgusted sigh. "You stay here 'n' make sure the prof doesn't turn into a bat an' fly away! See you later, John baby!"

And with that, Fergie took off, running. Imitating Father Higgins, he vaulted the turnstile and went galloping off into the gloom. Johnny watched him go. Now both of his friends had vanished into the night. Johnny felt the sick taste of fear rising in his throat. What if they were gone for good? What if something was swallowing up the people on this island, one by one? No, no—that couldn't possibly be! He was allowing his imagination to run away with him. Fidgeting and peering anxiously around, he limped back and forth in front of the chapel door. With each step he took, it felt as if somebody were shooting red-hot needles into his ankle.

Oh well, thought Johnny, *it'll take my mind off of the other stuff I'm worried about.* But he couldn't get rid of his worries that easily—as soon as he stopped walking, they came flooding back. Feverishly he went over in his mind things that could possibly have happened to Father Higgins. What if he had wandered into the ocean accidentally and had gotten drowned? Johnny was a very good worrier. He could dream up dozens of ghastly things that might have happened to Father Higgins. Minutes dragged past. The wind blew, and more rain pelted down. Johnny thought of the song the professor always sang when it was raining:

> When and that I was a little tiny boy
> With hey ho, the wind and the rain,
> A foolish thing was but a toy
> For the rain it raineth every day!
> With hey ho, the wind and the . . .

"Oh, come on, somebody!" Johnny yelled into the wind. *"Please, come back!"* No answer came. Johnny was in an agony of indecision. What should he do? If Fergie and Father Higgins were in trouble, shouldn't he go and rescue them? Around his neck he wore the silver crucifix with the fragments of the True Cross imbedded in it. This was what had saved him from a horrible death just a few short hours ago. It was hard to believe that Father Higgins had come out to this island with his pockets crammed full of sacred things that would ward off evil forces and demonic shapes. So maybe he, John Dixon, was the only one who could save the day. Maybe he ought to dash back to the boat. It wouldn't take long . . . or would it? He remembered his bad ankle. What if it was not just sprained but broken? What if he collapsed from the pain on the way to the boat? Hundreds of *what if*'s came leaping into Johnny's mind—he was so

nervous and frustrated and frightened that he wanted to scream. Unzipping his jacket, he reached inside and closed his hand around the lump of cloth that held the silver crucifix. . . .

And at that moment Johnny heard a sound behind him, a strange unearthly sound that was like the hinges of a hundred doors creaking and men and women and children groaning in agony. Johnny's hand relaxed its grip on the crucifix. Slowly he turned around. And what he saw gave him the shock of his life.

CHAPTER TEN

The chapel was gone. In its place stood a dignified old Victorian mansion with a mansard roof and deep-set attic windows. The ground-floor windows were long and had heavy drapes on the inside. The drapes reached all the way to the floor, and they had been pulled tight so that no glimmer of light could be seen. Over the front door was a fanlight, and flanking the stout oak portal were two flat pilasters with scrolled capitals on top. At Johnny's feet lay a semicircular slab of stone that served as a front stoop for the house. And on the stone lay little wandering white trails of *snow*. Johnny gasped. He staggered back, awestruck. And he saw, off to the left, a light shining. In a dreamlike trance, trembling and holding his breath, he moved around the corner of the house toward the lighted window—and then he got his second shock.

He found that he was peering in at a horribly familiar room. It was the dollhouse room, the one he had seen in his midnight vision at the Fitzwilliam Inn. There was the fireplace, the red Oriental rug, the built-in bookshelves, the table with the oil lamp and the Bible on it—everything. And in the black leather chair sat Professor Childermass. He was still dressed in his ragged shabby clothes, and he appeared to be asleep. His hands were folded in his lap, and Johnny could see his chest moving in and out as he breathed. Icy terror gripped Johnny's heart. This was the death room. Without being told, he somehow knew that a dark shape would soon appear in the doorway off to the right. The unearthly thing that had snuffed out Lucius Childermass's life would be returning, and it would put its hand over the professor's face, and . . .

"*No! No!*" yelled Johnny, and he rushed at the window. With all his might he banged and slammed on the glass. He pounded with his fists till his hands stung. But he might as well have been pounding on sheet metal, for all the good it did. The professor slept on, and the firelight flickered over the red carpet, and the pendulum on the mantel clock wagged. Johnny stumbled back, eyes goggling. Then blind panic seized him, and he turned and ran. He was at the bottom of the hill before he knew it, shoving his way through the creaking turnstile. On over the dark, rainy field he ran, limping badly. He never knew, afterward, how he managed to make it down to the shore. But he did, and only when he had stopped running did he gasp, because of the unbelievably fiery stinging. Madly Johnny looked around. There was the boat. Rain pelted down on the tarpaulin that had been thrown over the food and the other things. Nearby, under a tree that grew close to the shore, lay Father Higgins. As Johnny moved nearer, flashlight dangling from his limp hand, he saw a heavy tree limb that lay near the priest's inert body. Father Higgins didn't move a muscle. Was he dead?

Johnny stumbled closer and dropped to his knees. He played the beam of his flashlight on Father Higgins's head, and he saw a clotted sticky mass of blood in his hair. *Oh, please no!* Johnny prayed desperately. *Please no, not this, not this. . . .*

Father Higgins groaned. He opened his eyes and stared blearily up at Johnny. "We're surrounded," he mumbled thickly. "Pinned down . . . rifle fire . . . can't get out. Gotta take out those mortars! Got any grenades left? Here . . . lemme try."

If Johnny had been able to break down and cry, he would have. But as it was, he just felt numb. Father Higgins's mind was wandering back to the island of Guam, during the Second World War. Johnny put his hands over his face. "*What do I do now?*" he muttered through his fingers. They were all going to be killed, here on this little hunk of rock and sand. People would find their bodies weeks from now and wonder what had happened. Johnny wanted to give up. He wanted to throw his body down on the sand beside Father Higgins and just wait for the end. But with a violent effort he shook off despair. He was still alive, and he was *not* going to give up! Johnny dragged himself to his feet. He tried to force his weary brain to think calmly. Where was Fergie? He had come down to find Father Higgins, but apparently he had never made it. What could . . .

A twig snapped. Bushes rustled. Turning suddenly, Johnny peered off into the dark mass of bushes that loomed nearby, right at the edge of the beach. By straining his eyes he could just make out a shadowy human shape.

"Fergie?" Johnny called in a faltering voice. "Hey, Fergie, is . . . is that you?"

More crackling and snapping. The shape shuffled closer. Johnny felt a deathly chill, and the hairs on the back of his neck stood up. He had a sudden vision of the scarecrow thing that he had seen on the ferryboat. In a flash Johnny plunged his hand in under his shirt and gripped the silver crucifix. The shape halted. It hovered menacingly for a second or two, and then it melted back into the dark bushes. The chill passed away, and Johnny somehow knew that the thing was gone . . . for the time being.

And now what was he going to do? Johnny didn't know. He lifted the crucifix's chain off his neck and played the flashlight's pallid beam over this odd, magical object. At the place where the arms of the crucifix crossed was a tiny dome of glass, and under it were the two holy splinters. This blessed talisman could ward off evil, but it couldn't help him to rescue the professor. No, something else was needed for that. But what? Johnny wished that he was a sorcerer, with reams of powerful curses and incantations rolling around in his head. A great wizard like Albertus Magnus or Count Cagliostro would be able to fight magic with magic. But he was just John Michael Dixon, of 23 Fillmore Street, in Duston Heights, Massachusetts. What could . . .

And then a very odd, unlikely thought came floating into his mind. Father Higgins had told him once that some of the Latin phrases in the Mass were thought to have magical powers. Johnny was an altar boy, and he knew a lot of church Latin by heart. But there was a better source than his poor befogged brain—he would use Father Higgins's breviary, the little prayer book that he carried in his coat pocket. The breviary was full of prayers—some in English and some in Latin—and one of them just might do the trick for him. Once again Johnny knelt down. He took off his rain-soaked jacket and folded it up to make a pillow for Father Higgins's head. Then he fumbled in the right-hand pocket of the priest's clerical jacket. Nothing there but loose change. With a sinking heart Johnny tried the other pocket . . . and his hand closed over a small book. This was it! He had found it!

Johnny stood up and—limping badly—he began to make his way back toward the graveyard. But he had only taken a few steps when he stopped. An awful thought had come to him. What if the scarecrow thing —or whatever it was that had been hovering nearby— what if it came to get Father Higgins? Maybe it had been about to pounce on him when Johnny arrived. What if the blessed book, the breviary, had been the only thing that kept Father Higgins safe? He couldn't just leave him here with no protection at all. Reluctantly Johnny turned back. He reached into his pocket and pulled out the crucifix and chain. Kneeling, he gently slid the chain over the priest's neck. Once again Johnny shone his flashlight beam at Father Higgins's face. His eyes were closed, and he was mumbling something that Johnny couldn't make out. Johnny didn't want to leave him, but he had to. Muttering a prayer, he pulled himself to his feet and set out again.

The rain was stopping, and the clouds, driven by a strong wind, were breaking up. Johnny saw a vague silvery glow overhead, which meant the moon was trying to break through. It was easier to see now, and he forced himself to plod on over the bumpy field and up the little hill to the cemetery. He felt very jittery without the crucifix hanging around his neck. It was true that the breviary had been blessed—at least, Johnny hoped that it had. Father Higgins had told him once that all the sacred implements used by a priest—his Mass vestments, the chalice, and so on—had been blessed by a bishop. But would a blessed book save him? Johnny was in tears now. He was feeling sorry for the professor, for

Father Higgins, for Fergie, for himself. Through the creaking turnstile and up the cemetery road he stomped. Wearily he looked up and he saw the dark, unreal house still looming against the sky. Sniffling, Johnny came to a halt and put the flashlight under his armpit. Holding the book rigidly in both hands, he began to chant loudly:

Judica me, Deus et discerne causam·meam de gente non sancta; ab homo iniquo et doloso erue me.

If he expected the house to disappear, he was disappointed—it was still there. *This is crazy,* thought Johnny, *absolutely crazy!* He flipped a page and read more:

Suscipiat Dominus sacrificium de manibus suis, ad laudam et gloriam nominis tuae . . .

Johnny stopped reading. He stopped because a small cold glowing object had appeared on the page that he held before him. The skull. Grinning with malice, eyes lit by tiny red dots of fire, it hovered in the flashlight's pale beam. And a harsh, pitiless voice burst inside Johnny's brain: *No one will cheat me of my vengeance, which will be visited upon all, even the seventh son of the seventh son! Come, foolish child, and see what I have prepared, for the way of the transgressor is hard, and the lamp of the iniquitous shall be put out!*

Johnny's arms dropped to his sides. The book fell into the mud at his feet, and the flashlight rolled away down the hill. Jerked forward by an irresistible force, Johnny tottered up toward the phantom mansion. He was being led to the lighted window, and he was forced to stop. Invisible hands seized his shoulders and shoved him rudely forward until his face was almost touching the glass. He wanted to close his eyes, but he couldn't—he had to watch. The professor slept on, sunk into the deep leather armchair. And—as Johnny had feared—the scene that now began to unfold was just like the one he had seen in the dark, cold room in the Fitzwilliam Inn. The yellow flame in the oil lamp's chimney dwindled to a sputtering blue point. The flames in the fireplace wavered, shrank, died out. And as the door at the back of the room began to open, the shadowy form moved into the room. *No! No!* Johnny screamed, but the scream burst in his head. He couldn't yell or twitch his nose or move a muscle of his body. The thing was hovering over the professor, bending horribly close to him. The shadowy hand was creeping toward the professor's face. . . .

"*Aaaaaaaah!*"

The air was split by a loud, violent, bull-like bellowing. Up the road charged Father Higgins. In his hand he gripped the silver crucifix. He held it high over his head like a banner, and the chain clinked and shimmered in the air. The big priest's arm was around Johnny's shoulder now, and he felt the cold metal being pressed to his forehead. Suddenly he could move. Reeling backward, he turned and watched as Father Higgins dashed madly to the front door of the mansion, dropped to his knees, and laid the crucifix down on the stone doorstep. In a loud, angry, challenging voice he started chanting:

> I bind unto myself today
> The strong name of the Trinity
> With invocations of the same
> The Three in One, and One in Three!
> The bursting from the spicéd tomb
> The riding up the heavenly way
> The coming at the Day of Doom
> I bind unto myself today!

As soon as the last word of this incantation was out of Father Higgins's mouth, the solid-looking mansion began to waver and shimmer. It looked like something seen through the windshield of a car in the rain. And then it was gone, and in its place stood the dumpy boarded-up chapel. Silence. The moon slid out from behind a cloud, and a pale ray lit the front door of the chapel. Father Higgins knelt motionless, the silver cross clenched tight in his hand. Johnny could hear his heavy, labored breathing. There came a scuttering, crunching sound, and the chapel door was yanked inward. Professor Childermass stepped out over the doorsill. He looked dazed, and he glanced this way and that. Suddenly he saw Father Higgins kneeling in the mud in front of him, and he let out a joyful croaking yell.

"*Higgy!*" he screeched, rushing forward and throwing his arms around his friend. "*Higgy!* What on earth are *you* doing here? For that matter, what am *I* doing here? Eh? What's going on? And is that John over there? It is! John, you're all wet! Your grandmother will have a fit!"

The professor paused and looked down at the priest, who still knelt motionless before him. Father Higgins was crying now. Tears were streaming down his grizzly cheeks. But the professor was not feeling weepy—he was looking more and more annoyed by the second.

"For the love of Pete!" he roared. "Will *somebody please* tell me what the devil is going on?"

CHAPTER ELEVEN

Somehow the three of them made it back down to the shore. Johnny limped on his sprained ankle, and the professor helped Father Higgins, who was still feeling dizzy from the blow that he had taken on the head. When they got to the boat, they found Fergie sitting on the bow, looking dejected and confused. When he saw his three friends coming toward him, he really went wild— he gave football cheers and jumped and danced around. And finally, when he had calmed down a bit, he explained that he had been led into a thicket by somebody who looked like Father Higgins. Then whoever-it-was had disappeared, and Fergie had gotten totally lost. He had wandered out to the other end of the island, and by the time he got back to the boat, there was no one there at all. At this point, he'd felt so completely mixed up that he just sat down and decided to wait till somebody came to *him* for a change.

When he had finished his little tale, Fergie turned to Father Higgins with a puzzled frown on his face. "So, if it wasn't you, Father . . . then who the heck was I following?"

"Who indeed?" muttered the priest, smiling grimly. "I'll tell you this, though, Byron: *Divide and conquer* is an ancient maxim for those who want to grind others into the dust. But as for all the rest of the whys and whats and wherefores of this affair . . . well, I think we'll have to wait a bit before we can say anything." He put his hand to his head and winced. "Right now," he added with a painful grimace, "I think I could do with about six dozen aspirin. Or a slug or two of that brandy that I was going to use to get the professor hammered."

"Hammered?" said the professor, blinking in astonishment. "Higgy, what in *blazes* are you talking about?"

"I'll tell you later," said Father Higgins, chuckling. "In the meantime, let's get ourselves off of this rotten, cursed sand spit. And don't call me Higgy, Rod. You know I can't stand that!"

The four weary adventurers climbed into the motorboat. Father Higgins pulled the starter cord, and they were off at top speed, heading back toward Vinalhaven. When they got to the island, Father Higgins and the boys took the professor to the Lobster Pot Inn, where he had a hot bath and a much-needed shave. After he had gotten freshened up, the professor found—to his great surprise—that there were clean clothes and freshly shined shoes laid out for him. Father Higgins had taken them from the professor's house, using the key that the professor had left across the street with Grampa Dixon. There were clean pajamas too, and the professor undressed, put on the pajamas, and threw himself into the extra bed in Father Higgins's room. He was asleep in half a minute.

The next morning, while they were all waiting down at the dock for the ferryboat, Father Higgins told the professor all that he knew about the weird incidents that had led all of them on an expedition out to Cemetery Island. He explained about the Saint Anthony "messages," the skull, Johnny's midnight vision, and everything. The professor listened to all this calmly, and when Father Higgins was through, he snorted indignantly.

"Huh!" he muttered. "So some evil spirit decided that he was going to make mincemeat of me. And if this Warren Windrow hadn't scrawled one of his dream-thoughts down on the flyleaf of a book, I might not be standing here right now. The 'great reckoning,' the settling of accounts, would have happened to me! But there's still a lot in this business that is pretty murky. When I get home I'll have to see what I can do to clear things up."

"I think you oughta rest when you get home," suggested Johnny gently. He was afraid the professor would get sick if he exerted himself too much, after all he had been through.

"Rest, ha!" said the professor, glaring arrogantly around. "I never felt better or fitter in my life!"

When Professor Childermass got back to his gray stucco house on Fillmore Street, he found that things were in pretty much of a mess: several windows were broken, the aerial on the cupola was in danger of falling down, and the house was full of grime and dust. But with the help of Grampa Dixon, Johnny, Fergie, and some neighbors, he managed to get the old place fixed up in next to no time at all. And he found that his job at Haggstrum College was still waiting for him. Still, he kept wondering why he had gotten kidnapped in the first place. What forces of demonic magic had been at work? These and some other puzzling questions still remained, and so the professor decided to take a quick car trip up to his ancestral family home in Vermont. He rooted around in the attic, and since he belonged to a family that never threw anything away, he was able to find what he wanted. Not long after he got back, he announced to his friends that he was going to have a party to celebrate his return. A backyard cookout, no less.

And so, on a warm evening early in June, all of the professor's friends were gathered on the lawn behind his house. There were Gramma and Grampa Dixon, Father Higgins, Fergie and Johnny, and Professor Charles Coote of the University of New Hampshire, who was an expert on black magic. Professor Childermass had had some long-distance phone conversations with his old friend, and now he was planning to consult with him further so that some of the loose ends in this crazy business could be resolved.

The professor got all done up in one of his tasteless summer outfits: grass-stained khaki wash pants, a magenta short-sleeved shirt covered with yellow monkeys and guitars, a big apron with witty sayings all over it, and a puffy chef's hat. Then, with tight-jawed determination, he grilled hamburgers and hot dogs on the brick backyard stove that he had not used in at least fourteen years. He felt rather inept and clumsy, and he dropped more than one burger into the fire, but with the aid of lighter fluid and Father Higgins's expert advice about handling charcoal, he managed it all without once losing his temper.

Late in the evening the party goers were all sitting in lawn chairs talking quietly and sipping drinks.

"Now, then," the professor began in his best brusque, no-nonsense manner, "I suppose you'll all be wanting to know what I found out when I went up to Vermont to poke around in my ancestral attic."

"You had bloody well *better* tell us," said Professor Coote dryly, "or we'll roast you over what's left of the fire."

The professor harrumphed a bit and paced nervously back and forth puffing at his cigarette and blowing out little thin streams of smoke. Suddenly his face relaxed, and he smiled. "I suppose," he began, "that Higgy here has spilled the beans to those who weren't in on the hunt for me, and that therefore *everybody* knows that what happened had something to do with Warren Windrow, the man from Cemetery Island who was hanged because he tried to kill my dear old Granduncle Lucius. Are you all with me thus far?"

Everybody nodded, and some murmured *yeah*'s and *uh huh*'s.

"Good!" said the professor, and he began to pace again. "In order to fill in the missing pieces of this rather insane jigsaw puzzle, I took a little jaunt up to my ancestral home, where I rooted about in the attic. There had always been a story in the family that Uncle Lucius had kept a diary, but no one had ever seen it. So I poked about in his steamer trunk—the same one that had gone with him when he took a clipper ship to California and back—and I found the diary sewed up in the lining of the trunk. And imagine my surprise when I discovered that the secretive old cuss had written the diary in *classical Greek!*" The professor smiled in a self-satisfied way. "Little did Lucius know that his grandnephew would become a scholar and learn to read—"

"Oh, cut out the bragging, Roderick!" said Professor Coote, interrupting. "We all know you can read Greek! So *tell* us what you found out!"

The professor was somewhat taken aback, but he

recovered his composure and went on. "Hm . . . what I found out . . . yes, yes, of course! Hem! Well, to begin with, I discovered that Lucius was an even more unpleasant man than I had ever imagined he was. You see, after Windrow was hanged, Lucius bribed some officials so that he could have the body turned over to a small medical school in San Francisco. Medical students can always use fresh cadavers, which they dissect and dismember in various ghoulish ways. Well! Good old Lucius extracted from the doctors the promise that they would turn Windrow's skull over to him when they were finished with the body."

Gramma made an awful face. "His *skull*!" she exclaimed. "What kind of a man was your uncle, to do a thing like that?"

The professor wrinkled his nose. "He was a very vengeful and nasty man. Also possibly unbalanced. And he had read a lot of ancient history, and he was planning to do what the Scythians did with their enemies— namely, to make a drinking cup out of poor Windrow's skull. It would be the final humiliation of the man who had dared to lay murderous hands on him. But, alas, Lucius had bitten off more than he could chew. He didn't know anything about Warren Windrow's background. I didn't, either, until I started digging, but I discovered that the Windrows were a family of witches and warlocks. They lived all over the Penobscot Bay area, on Matinicus and Vinalhaven and in Thomaston and in Camden. And the reason why they kept moving around was this: They kept getting pitched out of wherever they were living because of their nefarious and diabolical practices.

"Ah, but good old Lucius knew nothing of this, so he put Windrow's skull in a hatbox and took it back with him. He went to live at our old place in Vermont, and the hatbox wound up on a shelf in his bedroom closet. Years passed, and oddly enough, Lucius never got around to making his Scythian drinking cup. However—as he records in his diary—he found that the skull obsessed him. He would take it out of its box every now and then, in the privacy of his room, and he would rub and caress it. He never seems to have understood why he did this. Weird, eh?"

"Hey, professor?" said Fergie, speaking up suddenly.

"Yes, Byron? What is it?"

"Didn't . . . well, I mean, didn't your uncle's family think it was kind of batty for him to keep somebody's skull in a hatbox in his room? Did any of them say anything about it to him?"

The professor shook his head. "No. They didn't know the skull was there. When Lucius showed up at the old homestead back in the mid–eighteen-fifties, everyone must've assumed that a hat was in the hatbox. And the old boy never let out a peep about his sordid little secret. Of course, they went through his belongings after his death, but . . . Well, I'm getting ahead of my story."

The professor paused to pull his burned-out cigarette butt from the jade holder. He stuck a new one in and lit it. "To continue," he went on, spewing clouds of smoke as he talked, "the years passed, and things did not go well with Lucius—I got this part of the tale from my father, since I was just a wee little kid when Lucius died. Everything he tried to do flopped, and in the end he became a gloomy hermit who spent a lot of time in his bedroom. On the evening of the day after Christmas, in 1883, Lucius died mysteriously. A few days later, when the members of the family opened his bedroom closet, and took the lid off the hatbox, guess what they found!"

"An empty hatbox?" suggested Johnny.

The professor shook his head solemnly. "No. Guess again!"

"I give up," said Johnny.

Fergie shrugged. "Okay, okay! It's a trick question. They found the skull, right?"

The professor's eyebrows rose, and he made a puckery face. "Well . . . yes and no. That is, they found the skull, but they didn't know they had found the skull."

"*Huh?*" said Fergie, gaping.

In a flash, Johnny guessed. "Oh, my God!" he exclaimed, and he clapped his hand over his mouth.

The professor turned to Johnny, and he made a little mock-courteous bow. "Go to the head of the class, young man! Yes, indeedy! What they found was a teeny-tiny skull, the same one that wound up on the shelf by the fireplace in the dollhouse room that some of us here have seen. You ask, how could this be? Well, remember,

Warren Windrow was a young warlock. And after he had gotten his revenge on Lucius, his evil, disembodied mind had thought up a way to pass on the curse. *Aaaand*, since no one in the Childermass family knew that a full-size skull had been in the hatbox, nobody guessed that the lovely delicate miniature was a real skull!"

Johnny turned very pale. Cold beads of sweat formed on his forehead, and he realized that everyone was looking at him. He felt ashamed and hung his head. "I . . . I should've got rid of it right away," he mumbled. "I mean, I shouldn't've picked it up in the first place."

The professor smiled and patted Johnny on the shoulder sympathetically. "Don't be too hard on yourself, John," he said softly. "The evil spirit of Warren Windrow probably intended for you to pick up the skull. And as you discovered later, it's not an easy matter to throw a thing like that away. But to continue with the story: Marcus Childermass—my father—took the skull away and kept it in his room, and, under its evil influence, he went to work on the Childermass clock. He'd had some experience in carpentry, so the idea wasn't totally—"

"Wait! Wait!" exclaimed Professor Coote, waving his hand in the air like a student who knows the answer. "I think I've discovered a hole in this story!"

The professor folded his arms and pretended to look annoyed. Then he unexpectedly burst out laughing. "Yes, I *know* you think you've found a hole, you insufferable pedant! But I'll plug it for you while you wait. You want to know how come my father didn't get blitzed by the power of Windrow's skull. And the answer is this—he never touched it. I mean, his fingers never actually came in contact with the filthy thing. I don't know for sure that this is the answer—I'm just guessing. But Dad was a meticulous, fussy man—a lot like this Mr. Finnick you folks have told me about, though I will hasten to add that my father was a good deal more warmhearted! Anyway, I think Dad must've handled the skull with tweezers, and that was what saved him. I, on the other hand, was not so lucky. My finger grazed the skull that night in the Fitzwilliam Inn, and it nearly got me killed. I'm just lucky I have such good, kind . . ." The professor's voice trailed off, and he turned away. He was crying now, and he tried to cover it up with a fit of coughing and harrumphing.

Professor Coote jumped up and ran to offer the professor his handkerchief. He took it and blew his nose several times, and he muttered something about Russian cigarettes. Then everybody got up and went to the card table that stood by the brick stove and poured themselves more drinks. For a while after that, the party goers just milled around and talked quietly.

At a little after ten o'clock, Gramma and Grampa announced that it was bedtime for them. They thanked the professor for the party and ambled on home, arm in arm. Johnny and Fergie discussed their narrow escape for a while, and then Fergie went into the house to use the bathroom, and Johnny drifted over to join the professor, Father Higgins, and Professor Coote. The three men had wandered down to the far end of the backyard to look at the sad remains of the professor's vegetable garden. He had been away during the spring planting season, and the plot of ground was just a weed-grown mess.

"By the way, Charley," said the professor, "are you *sure* Finnick didn't have anything to do with this business? I mean, it's a bit hard for me to believe that he and his museum just happened to be out on Vinalhaven, near the place where Warren Windrow lived. Isn't it possible that he's a member of the Windrow clan?"

Professor Coote shook his head. "No, I don't think it's likely. Finnick is a pretty detestable person, I gather, but that doesn't make him a sorcerer. As unlikely as it may seem, his being out on Vinalhaven is exactly what it seems to be—a ridiculous, insane coincidence."

The professor rubbed his chin and looked doubtful. "Well, Charley," he said slowly, "I know you're an expert on hocus-pocus and abracadabra, but still . . ."

"Professor Coote?" said Johnny, interrupting. "Could . . . could I ask you something?"

Professor Coote turned and smiled at Johnny. "Yes, John? You look upset. What is it?"

Johnny wrinkled up his forehead and bit his lip. "Well, I was just wondering . . . that is, do you think the curse of the skull and the dollhouse and Warren Windrow is over for good?"

Professor Coote sloshed the brandy in the snifter he was holding. Then he reached out and flicked some fluff off the top of a tall, stalky weed that was growing in the professor's garden. "I was afraid someone would ask me about that," he said in a grave, troubled voice. "And the answer is, I don't know for sure. I'm an expert on magic, but there is a lot I don't understand about it. However, I will say this: The curse was interrupted at the precise moment when it was supposed to have ripened. That is, Roderick here was to have been killed on the anniversary of the day and the hour when Warren Windrow met his end on the gallows. But at that point our friend Father Higgins here came charging in like a Notre Dame fullback, and he dispelled the curse by using the power of the True Cross, and one of the oldest, most potent incantations in the world. By the way, Tom, where on earth did you dig that piece of wizardry up? I know it in Celtic, and in Old Icelandic, but I wasn't aware that it had been translated into English."

Father Higgins sipped his whiskey and smiled. "It's part of an old hymn called 'Saint Patrick's Breastplate.' I've known it since I was a kid, but it never occurred to me that the thing might have magical properties until a couple of years ago. I was playing it over on the organ one night when nobody was in the church, and then it hit me, and I said to myself, *This isn't a hymn, this is a charm!* And darned if I wasn't right!"

Johnny swallowed hard. "You mean . . . you mean you didn't know it would work when you came chargin' up the hill to save us?"

Father Higgins shook his head. "I most certainly did *not*! I felt like it was two out in the ninth, and I was comin' to bat with a toothpick in my hands. But we must never underestimate the power of invocations to the Blessed Trinity."

"Or the power of ancient Irish superstitions," Professor Coote added, chuckling. "You see, John, magic is a rather uncertain science—or as some would have it, a pseudoscience. So to finish what I was saying earlier, if you and Roderick here will just manage to stay away from Cemetery Island for the rest of your lives, I don't think there'll be any problem."

"Don't worry," muttered the professor as he sipped his sherry. "I'll give the place a wide berth! As for this summer, I plan to hang around Duston Heights and work on my golf game and listen to all the Red Sox broadcasts. In fact, I'll probably spend so much time with my ear glued to the radio that I'll never get my new book written."

"Book?" said Johnny innocently. "I didn't know you were writing a book, professor."

The professor glared. "Of *course* I'm writing a book— or rather, I was, until I got whisked off to that island paradise off the coast of Maine. You remember the book, Charley. The one on the causes of the Napoleonic Wars."

"Ah, yes!" said Professor Coote, grinning mischievously. "*That* book! Well, Roderick, if you don't get it finished, it'll be a small loss. After all, who would ever want to read it?"

"*Whaaaaat?*" roared the professor, waving his burning cigarette. "Do you *dare* to insinuate that I, Roderick Childermass, Ph.D., could ever write a dull . . ."

And, still crabbing and cranking good-naturedly, the professor began walking slowly up toward the house in the company of his friends.

JOHN BELLAIRS

is the critically acclaimed, best-selling author of many Gothic novels, including *The Treasure of Alpheus Winterborn; The Curse of the Blue Figurine; The Mummy, the Will, and the Crypt; The Spell of the Sorcerer's Skull; The Revenge of the Wizard's Ghost; The Eyes of the Killer Robot;* and *The Dark Secret of Weatherend.*

A resident of Haverhill, Massachusetts, Mr. Bellairs is currently at work on another chilling tale.